'As a wife...billionaire, I'...

They stared at each other, and it became a prickly, tense, heart-stopping moment.

'Do you mean in bed?' Reith queried at last, with a significant scan up and down her figure.

'Now, that,' Kim said, 'might depend on you—*if* it happens. What I mean is that I will run your homes beautifully, I'll handle the entertaining, I'll look the part and...' she paused '...I'm good with kids.'

Reith said slowly, 'I've got an apartment in Bunbury. I'll lease it to your parents rent-free and I'll set up an allowance for them—for as long as you stay with me, Kim.'

She drew a breath. 'You drive a hard bargain.'

'You're not exactly playing softball yourself,' he said.

Lindsay Armstrong was born in South Africa, but now lives in Australia with her New Zealand-born husband and their five children. They have lived in nearly every state of Australia, and have tried their hand at some unusual occupations, such as farming and horse-training—all grist to the mill for a writer! Lindsay started writing romances when their youngest child began school and she was left feeling at a loose end. She is still doing it and loving it.

In 2011, Lindsay's book THE SOCIALITE AND THE CATTLE KING won a R*BY award in the 'Short Sexy' category.

Recent titles by the same author:

THE GIRL HE NEVER NOTICED
THE SOCIALITE AND THE CATTLE KING
ONE-NIGHT PREGNANCY
THE BILLIONAIRE BOSS'S INNOCENT BRIDE

WHEN ONLY DIAMONDS WILL DO

BY

LINDSAY ARMSTRONG

First published in Great Britain 2012
by Mills & Boon, an imprint of Harlequin (UK) Limited.
Harlequin (UK) Limited, Eton House, 18-24 Paradise Road,
Richmond, Surrey TW9 1SR

ISBN: 978 0 263 89113 3

Harlequin (UK) policy is to use papers that are natural, renewable and recyclable products and made from wood grown in sustainable forests. The logging and manufacturing process conform to the legal environmental regulations of the country of origin.

Printed and bound in Spain
by Blackprint CPI, Barcelona

WHEN ONLY DIAMONDS WILL DO

PROLOGUE

REITH RICHARDSON slammed his phone down and swore beneath his breath.

His secretary, Alice Hawthorn, grey-haired and in her fifties, raised her eyebrows. 'Francis Theron, I gather?'

'You gather right,' Reith agreed. 'He doesn't believe I'm a suitable person to be—' he paused and grimaced '—within a hundred miles of his beloved winery, no doubt. Despite the fact he's in dire straits, despite the fact my offer is the only one he's got and he could end up bankrupt in the near future.'

'Hmm…' Alice mused. 'A very socially prominent family, the Therons of Balthazar and Saldanha. Very proud.'

'You know what they say about pride and the proverbial fall,' Reith murmured. 'OK, Alice, I'm withdrawing the offer I made. I'll leave the Therons to their fate.' He bundled the papers before him into a stack and handed them over to her.

'There's a daughter, you know,' Alice said, as she

packed the papers into a folder. 'An absolute stunner, I believe. About twenty-two.'

Reith shrugged. 'Maybe they need to find her a rich husband who can save them all.'

'There's also a son.'

'I know, I've met him—all the right schools, top polo player, seriously into horses, in fact, but singularly unblessed with any business sense,' Reith replied dryly then he smiled a crooked grin. 'Maybe they need to find *him* a horsy but rich wife.'

Alice laughed and got up. 'Will you be in Perth or Bunbury for the next few days?'

'Bunbury, probably, there's a stud down that way I'm interested in. Alice,' Reith said with a frown as he looked around his office, one of his new luxury suite of offices in Perth that overlooked the Swan River, 'I don't like the artwork the interior decorator's supplied. I don't know why, it just doesn't do anything for me.'

Alice looked around at the Impressionist landscapes and marine life on the walls. 'Well, perhaps you ought to choose it yourself?' she suggested.

Reith got up and strolled over to the windows. 'All right, when I get the time,' he said wryly. 'Thanks, Alice.'

She took the hint but when she got back to her desk she sat deep in thought for a while. It wasn't often her boss backed a wrong hunch—made an offer that was knocked back, in other words. In fact his timing was usually impeccable and he was little short of a genius when it came to buying businesses in trouble and turning them around. It was how he'd consolidated a small fortune made from a mining venture into a very large fortune, but this was obviously different. This was something that involved pride and history; the Therons went back a long way to their Huguenot ancestors in South Africa and viticulture ran in their veins.

Whereas Reith Richardson went back to a cattle station beyond the black stump…

Alice shrugged and patted the folder she was about to file away for the last time. Concerning her boss, there were times when she fervently wished herself twenty years younger, and other times when she felt rather motherly. This was one of those motherly times, she decided. A time when she wished he would be a little more understanding, a little less the steel-hard businessman.

What he really needed, she mused, was a softening influence in his life, like a wife. And heaven knew there were plenty of women who found his tall, dark looks fascinating but of course his disinclination to marry any of them could be due to the fact that he had lost his first wife.

Alice stopped her thoughts at this point as her phone rang and she was completely unaware that, at the same time, her boss was staring at a framed photo on his desk and thinking about his lost wife.

It wasn't a photo of his wife but a boy, a freckled, fair boy who went by the name of Darcy Richardson. His only son, his only child. Born of a girl who had been little more than a child herself except in years. She'd been nineteen when they'd married because she was pregnant, twenty when she'd given birth to Darcy and died from unforeseen complications.

And he very much doubted he'd ever get over the guilt he felt. Guilt because it had all happened so quickly. He'd never expected a pregnancy but he should have sensed that she was being naïve when she claimed she was protected; a country girl who'd stopped taking the Pill when it made her sick. But most of all guilt over her dying—as if he'd caused it.

And now the guilt over Darcy, his son, who'd been mostly brought up by his maternal grandmother until six months ago when she'd died. Darcy, who wore a polite protective shell around him that he, his father, could not get through.

Darcy, who was coming soon from his boarding school, not only to remind his father of his mother, who he looked a lot like—not that he knew it—but also to be the perfect guest in his own home.

Reith Richardson dug his hands into his pockets and breathed savagely. Give him sterile business relationships rather than complicated, tense, still-waters-run-deep, personal relationships any day.

And thinking of that led him to think of Frank Theron and what he'd said on the phone… *Not only have I got my family to think of but I've got my pride...*

You'd be better to concentrate on your family and forget about your pride, Mr Theron, he reflected, much better. And his expression hardened as he thought of Francis Theron and his son Damien…

CHAPTER ONE

'LADY—are you *mad*?'

A complete stranger said this as he got out of his car. He was breathing heavily.

There was dust swirling around them, dust raised when the stranger, in response to her signal for help, had almost driven his car into a large tree. He'd only corrected the situation at the last moment. The car was a late model gun-metal luxury four-wheel drive.

'I'm sorry,' she said hastily. 'My name is Kimberley Theron and I'm in a dreadful hurry but the thing is I appear to have run out of petrol. Would you be able to help?'

'Kimberley Theron?' the man she was addressing repeated.

'You may have heard of...well, not me so much but the name?' She looked at him searchingly, and her eyes suddenly widened.

Talk about tall, dark and handsome—no, not handsome; that was too bland a way to put it—rugged and interesting said it much better, she decided. He looked to be in his middle thirties. He was tanned with wide shoulders and an admirable physique beneath cargo pants and a grey sweatshirt. He had dark eyes and short dark hair.

'Kimberley Theron,' he repeated and studied her comprehensively from top to toe, then her silver convertible, its cream leather upholstery now coated with dust. 'Well, Miss Theron, has no one—' he folded his arms across his chest '—ever told you that dancing into the road pulling up your skirt and exposing your legs could cause…chaos?'

'Actually—' she paused for a moment and screwed up her forehead '—no one ever thought to mention that!' She looked down at her legs, now demurely clothed beneath her denim skirt. She looked up and her sapphire-blue eyes were laughing. 'I am sorry,' she said contritely, however. 'But I guess there is a funny side to it. I really couldn't think of any other way to make *sure* you stopped.'

He didn't look amused. He swore beneath his breath instead and looked around. It was a country road with lion-coloured paddocks running along either side of it. There was no sign of any habitation in either direction; there was absolutely no sign of any traffic. The sun was beating down.

He said, 'I can't siphon off any fuel for you because I run on diesel; you don't. Where are you going?'

'Bunbury. Are you— You *are* going in the right direction. Is there any chance I could get a lift with you?'

The stranger looked Kimberley Theron up and down again. Early twenties, he guessed, and she *was* stunning, with red-gold hair, those sapphire eyes, a good figure, not to mention, he thought dryly, sensational legs.

There was also an innate liveliness to her you couldn't mistake, even if she had just about caused you to collide with a very big tree.

There was more, though. Behind the liveliness and whimsical humour lurked a...what was it?...an unshakeable conviction that she was no mere mortal—she was a Theron! And, consequently, begging a lift from a complete stranger posed no hazards.

He grimaced. 'All right, but are you just going to leave it here?' He gestured to her car.

'No.' She hesitated. 'Here's the other thing, my phone has run out of battery. Would you have a mobile on you? And, if so, could I borrow it to call home and get them to come and pick the car up? I would pay for the call, naturally. And, naturally, I would pay for the petrol to get to Bunbury.'

'You don't have to—'

'I insist,' she told him with an imperious little toss of her head.

He looked at her then shrugged and pulled his phone out of his pocket and handed it to her. Moments later he was treated to a one-sided Theron to Theron conversation.

'Hello, Mum, it's Kim. Darling, be an angel...'

And there followed all the details of Kim Theron's predicament, plus the indication that she wasn't completely impractical as she gave a short but accurate description of his car, including the registration number. Then she ended the call and handed his phone back to him with a rueful expression.

'Sorry, I hope you didn't mind me giving my mother some details about you, but she's a worrier.'

He looked at her ironically.

'And that explains that, so I don't have to feel completely stupid!' she went on. 'My mother borrowed my car and neglected to replace the petrol she used. I didn't even think to check the gauge because I was in such a rush.'

'Why are you in such a rush?' he enquired.

'Can I tell you as we go along?'

He hesitated briefly, then gestured for her to get in.

'My friend Penny,' she said, settling herself into the passenger seat and doing up her seat belt, 'one of my best friends, is pregnant and the baby is—*was* due in a fortnight but she's gone into labour this morning. Her mother's in Melbourne—other side of the continent—her husband's driving a barge out from Port Hedland. She has no one else and it's her first baby.'

'I see,' he said. 'Did it cross your mind, once you'd phoned home, to wait for one of your family to come and rescue you?'

She shook her head. 'Saldanha, where I live, I mean, is half an hour's drive the *other* way and by the time they'd organized things—' she gestured expressively '—I could have lost hours.' She turned to him. 'Do you *mind* doing this?'

He changed gear to negotiate a sharp bend and wondered what she'd say if he told her that the last person he'd wanted to meet was a member of the Theron family of Saldanha and Balthazar…

'I was going to Bunbury anyway,' he said.

Kim watched him for a long moment, then, 'What's your name?'

'Reith.'

'That's unusual. What is it? Welsh?'

'No idea.' He shrugged.

'How strange,' Kim murmured.

He flicked her another ironic little glance. 'I suppose you know exactly where your name comes from?'

'As a matter of fact, I do,' she said gravely, although her eyes were sparkling. 'I was named after a diamond mine.'

'That's—' he paused '—curiously appropriate.'

'What does that mean?' Kim queried.

'You look like a diamond kind of girl.'

'I'm so glad you didn't say I look like the kind of girl whose best *friends* are diamonds,' she responded and tossed her red-gold hair. But she went on, apparently not seriously offended, 'Want to know which diamond mine?'

'Let me guess. The Kimberley mine in South Africa.'

'Got it in one! You are clever…er…Reith. Not a lot of people—in Australia—know about Kimberley in South Africa although, of course, a lot of them know about the Kimberley area up north, also associated with diamonds.'

He said nothing.

'May I borrow your phone again?' she requested then. 'I could ring the hospital and find out how things are going.'

* * *

Things were going apace at the hospital and Kim was blinking rapidly as she ended the call. 'I'll be lucky to get there in time!'

'Hold on,' he recommended.

She held on and the next ten minutes were breathless until they hit the outskirts of Bunbury and finally made the hospital.

'Thanks so much,' she panted. 'I—'

'Just go.' He gestured.

'Wait here, though,' she ordered, 'I'll get the news. At least you deserve to know if everything's all right. Besides I owe you some money.' And she flung herself out of the car and up the hospital stairs.

Reith Richardson grimaced, hesitated for a moment then put his car into gear and was about to drive off when Kim reappeared and danced down the steps.

'Seven pounds, ten minutes ago, a boy, mother and son are both fine—' she beamed through the window '—and I can't thank you enough. However, here's the thing, I can't *pay* you because I forgot to bring any money!'

'I never expected to be paid for a couple of lousy phone calls, so forget it, Miss Theron.'

'Well, I wish I could but I didn't bring anything, actually.'

He stared at her. 'You mean—no credit cards, no cash card?'

'Nothing,' she said ruefully. 'Not that it'll be a problem when my car arrives—but I just would love to take some flowers with me when I'm allowed in to see Penny. They have a florist here but—'

She stopped as Reith reached into his pocket and pulled out a hundred dollars.

'Oh, thank you so much! But look, I need your address so I can repay you.' She fished in her pocket and brought out a scrap of paper and a pen.

Reith Richardson opened his mouth to tell her to forget it again, but he changed his mind as he put the money into her hand. 'Have dinner with me, only if you feel like it.' He named a restaurant and a time and, as she stepped back looking thoroughly surprised, he drove off.

At ten to seven that evening he was sitting at a table for two in a luxury restaurant that overlooked the bay. It was a blue and tinsel evening, deep blue sky and water through the wide windows, silver-white patterned moon looming in the sky.

Rather than the moon, he was contemplating the beer he'd ordered and a few other things. Would Kimberley Theron take up his invitation? Why had he issued it in the first place? Was there something about her that intrigued him—obviously, he thought impatiently—but what was it?

Her looks, her body, her legs? Had to be more than that…

'Penny for them?' the object of his thoughts murmured as she pulled out the chair opposite.

He stood up and had to smile in admiration.

She'd changed from her denim skirt and cotton blouse into a dusty-pink linen dress, sleeveless and round-necked, which she wore with a string of bauble-sized glass beads and emerald cork-soled platform sandals. Her hair was loose and casual and a pair of diamond earrings nestled in the red-gold strands.

She looked sensational but she also looked different, a more mature—no, that was the wrong word, he decided—a more sophisticated version of Kimberley Theron.

She slid into her chair with a sigh of relief, looked appreciatively at the moisture-dappled bottle of champagne in an ice bucket and said, 'How nice. Nice to sit down, nice to think of a deliciously cool glass of bubbly. Today,' she added as he sat down, 'has been one of my wackier days.'

He poured her champagne. 'Wacky? How are mother and son, by the way?'

'They really are fine, despite his early arrival. And despite me arriving too late—not your fault,' she hastened to assure him. 'Wacky? Yes. When I got Penny's call, she sounded so lost and scared I just dropped everything and...well—' she smiled at him '—you know the rest of it. Incidentally—' she reached into her purse and withdrew a hundred-dollar note, which she slid across the table towards him '—thank you so much.'

He let it lie on the table.

'I gather you've got your resources back?'

She nodded. 'Yes, my car got delivered to the hospital so I was able to go home and change, et cetera.' She sipped her champagne. 'Mmm... Delicious. Tell me something, Reith—what do you do?'

'This and that.'

She looked comically askance at him but she was

frowning. He'd changed his cargo pants and sweatshirt for jeans, a navy shirt open at the throat and a beautifully cut finest tweed sports jacket. And he wore a sports watch that would have cost a small fortune. All in all, he looked right at home in this very expensive restaurant, not to mention darkly attractive.

'That sounds rather evasive.' She traced the rim of her glass with one slender finger as she withdrew her senses from the masculine onslaught of the man and thought of his answer to her question.

'It's also true.' He shrugged. 'I specialize in buying and rescuing companies in trouble.'

Kim frowned. 'What's the appeal in that?'

He studied her for a long moment. 'What do you mean?'

'Well, usually one has a vocation; you're drawn to medicine or law or farming or something.'

'It's the challenge,' he said. 'It's always a learning curve but some business principles, supply and demand, for example, always stand whether you're dealing with fashion or minerals or sheep. What do you do?'

She took another sip of champagne and looked thoughtful. 'I teach. English,' she said and smiled at his expression. 'Thought that might surprise you,' she murmured.

He grimaced. 'Why?'

'Why did I think it would surprise you? I get the feeling you don't approve of me, Mr...um...Reith.' She eyed him with a glimmer of wry humour in her blue eyes. 'It's quite a strong feeling,' she added gently.

'You did nearly cause me to wipe myself out,' he reminded her.

She laughed. 'Yes, well, I've already confessed to having a…an unusual kind of day. I'm generally a much more organized person.'

His lips twitched and he shrugged.

Kim planted her elbows on the table and rested her chin in her hands. 'You couldn't have said it more eloquently if you'd actually spoken the words.'

He raised his eyebrows. 'What?'

'You find that hard to believe?'

'I…'

Kim sat back and interrupted. 'Not that I mind. We're a bit like ships in the night, aren't we?'

He didn't answer, merely studied her.

'Would you mind if we ordered dinner?'

'Not at all.'

'That's the other thing I messed up today,' she confided. 'I haven't had a thing to eat since breakfast. And do you mind if I order lobster? I always have lobster here; I can thoroughly recommend it.'

'Be my guest,' he murmured.

'Oh, I wouldn't dream of it. It's not cheap so I insist on paying for my dinner. Actually, I'd like to pay for yours too!'

As a way of cutting me down to size? Reith wondered. As a way of being a Theron and making others aware that they're not quite in the same class?

'As a way of saying thank-you for the lift today and for lending me money for flowers and suggesting dinner,' Kim murmured.

Their gazes clashed.

Had she read his mind? he wondered, then became aware of a resolve forming within him that he didn't think he'd be able to ignore—he wanted this girl in his bed; he wanted to find out how she liked being made love to, whether she was still a Theron to her fingertips when she was hot and excited and writhing beneath him.

'Do you surf?'

They were out in the cooling night air, strolling towards the car park, when Reith asked the question.

'Of course,' Kim said without hesitation.

'Of course?' he queried, glancing down at her with some irony.

She paused and looked up. She wasn't short, five feet six, plus her wedges tonight, which meant he had to be well over six feet, and a little frisson ran through her because he was not only tall but beautifully proportioned…

But why that look of irony? she wondered.

'Have I said something wrong?'

He took her hand and swung it. 'No, I suppose not.'

'Now come on, tell me,' she insisted.

He stopped walking and turned her to face him but it was a long moment before he replied. In fact as his gaze roamed up and down her figure then lingered ruefully on her legs, Kim experienced another frisson but this one seemed to sizzle between them.

Then he shrugged and said, 'It's just that I get the feeling you do everything well—ride, swim, surf, play tennis, play the piano, draw or paint, speak fluent—something or other and—'

'Stop!' She held up her free hand. 'You're having a go at me, aren't you? You still think I'm rich and idle, despite the fact that I work.'

He rubbed his jaw reflectively. 'Not idle, no, but for the rest of it, you have the sort of assurance that leads one to suspect you of attending a good finishing school. Do you do any of those things?'

'I...' Kim closed her mouth and shrugged resignedly. 'I do swim and surf. I ride. I don't play the piano but I do play the harp, I do play tennis, I do speak fluent Spanish—but I do not draw or paint!' she finished triumphantly. 'Mind you, I have a good eye for art,' she confessed. 'But, tell me this, what's it all got to do with surfing?'

'Should we go down to Margaret River for a surf tomorrow?' He paused. 'The weather forecast is good and the swell is up.'

Kim's lips parted and her eyes lit up. 'I can think of nothing nicer, Mr—what *is* your name?'

His eyes narrowed for no reason she could detect. 'Richardson,' he said and waited a moment. 'Reith Richardson.'

'Well, Mr Richardson, I'd love to! I haven't surfed for a while.'

'And you can just take off from your teaching job when and wherever?' he queried.

'Oh, no, but I have time off at the moment. I did some overtime in the boarding house.' She raised her eyebrows. 'Where shall we meet?'

'Would you mind driving down to Busselton?'

'No-o,' Kim said slowly.

He swung her hand. 'I have a very early appointment down there—it would save me driving back. We can go on in one car.'

'Sure,' she said easily.

He lifted her hand and kissed her knuckles.

Kim swallowed as a tremor of pure physical attraction towards this tall, dark, rugged stranger ran through her. But he didn't feel like a stranger any more, although she didn't know much more about him than she'd known earlier in the day.

Well, she knew he preferred steak to lobster, beer to champagne, that his hands were clean and scrubbed but scarred and callused as if he'd done plenty of physical work at some time or another. Yet he sounded educated and well-read.

He released her hand as they reached her car. 'Try not to lure any more men to their doom against large, immovable objects, Miss Theron,' he advised as she unlocked the driver's door.

She laughed, 'I won't!'

'Oh, and this.' He took her purse from her and tucked her hundred-dollar note into it.

'But—'

'I'd like to pay for the flowers, that's all. Goodnight.'

'You know—' Kim stared up at him '—I've got the feeling you're quite addicted to getting your own way.'

'I have been accused of that, yes,' he agreed gravely. 'It's nonsense, of course.' He paused. 'On the other hand, we could be two of a kind.'

'Do you think so?' Kim asked wryly. 'That could make for some uncomfortable times between us, assuming we last any kind of distance. Goodnight.'

His lips twitched. 'It could. Yes, it could. Goodnight.'

Kim drove home in a thoughtful mood.

The moon was silvering the familiar landscape, so it wasn't familiar any more but an exotic surround with secretive dark patches.

Of course, she knew it off by heart but, thinking of how secretive and unknown in the moonlight it looked now, her thoughts took off down another path. Was she entering an unknown period of her life?

How could she be as affected as she was by a man she'd only just met? There was no doubt he sent shivers down her spine—shivers of pleasure. One light kiss on her knuckles had not only raised goose bumps for her but it had caused her to warm to him as if they could be friends who cared for each other.

Or was that being extremely fanciful? she asked herself as she swung into the driveway of the estate called Saldanha, the place she had always called home.

Set against the background of the Darling Range foothills, Saldanha was special. The Harvey and Margaret River districts south of Perth in Western Australia were beautiful and diverse, with their white beaches, jarrah forests, sleek cattle and the sheer fertility that produced glorious gardens. And adjacent to Saldanha was the Balthazar Winery, also owned by her parents—the other, and probably most famous, export of the area that grew premium grapes was wine.

Both Saldanha and Balthazar—a Balthazar was a

twelve-litre wine bottle—were the names brought by the Theron family, of Huguenot descent, from South Africa to the similar conditions and climate around Perth. The Theron family had also brought their viticulture skills and the Balthazar Winery had flourished. At the same time Saldanha, named after a sheltered bay north of Cape Town, had flourished and the Cape Dutch–style architecture of the house, white gables and a thatched roof, had become distinctive in the district.

So had the classic dry white that Balthazar was famous for as well as its Cellar Door, run on the estate and visited by wine-lovers from all over the world.

It was none of this Kim Theron was thinking of as she parked her car, greeted her dog, a devoted blue heeler that went by the name of Sunny Bob, and let herself into the darkened house.

Her parents were out and her brother no longer lived at home, although he kept his horses there, and the housekeeper had taken the opportunity to visit family.

But, as she switched on some lamps and kicked off her shoes, Kim's thoughts were still firmly centred on Reith Richardson.

Was it unusual to suggest they go surfing? she wondered. Perhaps, but a great idea nonetheless.

She paused at the foot of the stairs as she tried to analyse her emotions. She was intrigued, without a doubt. But, of course, as the saying went: look before you leap…

She had no idea, as she stood with her hand on the banister, how that phrase was going to come back to haunt her.

* * *

Margaret River was beautiful.

The peaceful river gave its name to a district that stretched between two capes—Cape Naturaliste and Cape Leeuwin—and ran inland as well. The town of Margaret River was not the only one in the area; there were quite a few, from Busselton to Yallingup and Cowaramup and more. There were some magnificent kauri forests as well as some fascinating limestone caves. The whole district was renowned not only for its wine but also its cuisine.

It was straight to the beach that Reith Richardson steered his four-wheel vehicle, though, after he'd collected Kim from their appointed meeting place in Busselton, along with her surfboard—and her dog.

'Hope you don't mind,' Kim said as she introduced them. 'Reith, this is Sunny Bob, and this, Sunny Bob,' she said to the blue heeler sitting politely at her feet, 'is Reith. He's a friend.'

'How do you do,' Reith said gravely but with his lips twitching as he patted the dog. 'Is he for protection—or what?'

'Oh, no!' Kim denied. 'Well, if the need ever arose—' She gestured and shrugged. 'But no, he loves the sea and he loves going out with me.'

Reith studied her for a moment. She wore colourful knee-length board shorts and a shocking pink bikini top under a string vest. Her hair was tied back and her beautiful designer sunglasses alone would have cost a small fortune.

'You look the part,' he commented as he transferred

her board across, then looked at what was left in her boot. 'What's all this?'

'I thought as much,' Kim replied with a mischievous grin. 'You're a typical iron-man surfer with no thought of creature comforts. You can put it all in your car,' she directed.

'But—'

'There's only a sun umbrella, a couple of folding chairs and a cooler with food and beverages. What's wrong with that?' she asked, with her hands planted on her hips.

He grimaced, then grinned. 'Nothing, I guess. I was going to drive us somewhere for lunch.'

'Perish the thought,' she said and looked around. 'On a perfect day like this, who wants to leave the beach?'

Several hours later, Reith, with a beer in one hand and a chicken drumstick in the other, said, 'You're a genius. How did you know cold roast chicken, beer—or, in your case, wine—go down perfectly after a surf?'

Kim giggled. 'Anyone knows that.' She lay back in her folding chair and sipped her wine. Sunny Bob lay contentedly beside her, having had an energetic few hours chasing waves whilst Kim and Reith had had a magnificent surf. He had his own bowl of cool fresh water.

She'd wrapped a pink sarong around her before she'd set out lunch. The sun was just starting to slide down from its zenith and there were a few wispy clouds trailing across the sky. The tide was out now so the roar of the surf was muted but you could still taste the salt in the air and feel the prickle of it on your skin. And it was hot and still, apart from some cicadas in the bush behind the beach.

'Why did you suggest this?' Kim's question seemed to pop out of nowhere.

'Why not?'

She hesitated. 'It just seems unusual for a businessman—look, I'm not complaining,' she said with a grin, 'but think barristers, stockbrokers, CEOs, medical men and you tend to spend a lot of time going out to dinner or cocktail parties or nightclubs or the theatre. Occasionally you may get a day out on a yacht or a day at the races but they're often too busy making money even to do that.'

'I spend a lot of time working behind a desk these days. Whereas I used to—' He paused.

'Go on. Used to—?' she prompted.

'Work on cattle stations, then I was a miner.'

'I wondered about that.'

He looked at her. 'Is it so obvious?'

'No,' she said slowly. 'It was your hands.'

He looked at his hands and grimaced. 'Anyway, I love the sea—most people who don't get to see it until their teens do—and it's good exercise.'

'So you grew up inland?'

'Yep.' He stared out over the ocean and for a moment there was an intensity to his dark gaze that made her frown and believe that he did love it. 'And beyond the black stump, speaking metaphorically,' he added.

Kim smiled. 'Are you married?'

He stirred. 'What makes you think that?'

'All the best ones are, according to Penny.' She pushed herself up against the back of her chair, bent her knees and smoothed her sarong over them. 'What kind of answer is that—are you or aren't you?'

'I'm not. I once was but she passed away.'

Kim sat up, looking appalled. 'You mean she died? What from?'

He nodded. 'A rare complication in childbirth.'

'Is… Did the baby survive?'

'Yes. His name's Darcy and he's ten now.'

Kim lay back. 'I'm sorry—very sorry.'

'Thanks,' he said briefly, then smiled slightly. 'What will Penny make of that?'

Kim shrugged. 'Put you in a special category, I guess.'

'How did I come up, anyway?'

Kim looked a touch embarrassed. 'I went to see her this morning before I drove down to Busselton. Naturally, I told her why I was dressed for the beach,' she said.

'Naturally.'

'Oh, look—' Kim closed her eyes '—ever since Penny got married she's been trying to sell me the state of matrimony as if it's the only state of bliss on the planet. Mind you, that doesn't stop her from warning me of the folly of falling for married men.'

'I think I get the drift,' he replied seriously.

Kim tossed him an annoyed little glance. 'Somehow you've made me feel about twelve,' she said crossly. Then her lips twitched. 'Penny and I have known each other since we were six so we're pretty close. And I suppose pretty girlish at times. But it's not girlish to want to know… Look, it doesn't matter.' She got up suddenly, stripped off her sarong and ran out from beneath the shade of the umbrella and across the hot sand to where the tide was tracing silvery crescents of foam on the damp sand.

And, barking joyfully, Sunny Bob streaked along beside her. The last to join her as she splashed in the shallows was Reith Richardson.

'You know,' he said, 'I would actually like to meet your Penny.'

'Why?' Kim stood still and stared at him.

'If it hadn't been for her I wouldn't have met you. Besides, maybe I could put her mind at rest.'

She eyed him but if he was laughing at her, he was hiding it well. There was no hiding, however, the streamlined strength of his body. He was lightly tanned and beautifully proportioned and she had to turn away suddenly as her breath caught in her throat at the thought of being in his arms.

She felt his hand on her and she looked over her shoulder and up at him.

It was a long, sober look they exchanged but it sent tremors of excitement and danger coursing through Kim's body because, in no uncertain terms, it told her that this man wanted her. She could see it in the way his gaze lingered on her breasts, her slim bare waist, her legs. Then he looked back into her eyes.

She licked her lips and curled her hands into fists because she desperately wanted to touch and be touched intimately, but Sunny Bob chose that moment to break the 'moment'. He raced up and threaded his way between them, and stayed there.

'Saved by the bell,' Reith murmured as he removed his hand.

Her eyes widened. 'Sunny Bob?'

'I get the feeling I'm on notice. Behave or else.'

Kim had to smile. 'Well—obviously,' she hastened to assure him, 'I wouldn't allow him to attack you.'

'Thank you,' he said formally, 'but having narrowly escaped death on the road because of you, I don't think I'll take any more risks. Do you dance?'

She turned round with a frown. 'Of course I dance! What's that got to do with anything?'

'Silly question,' he murmured. 'Do you take Sunny Bob out dancing with you?'

'Of course *not*,' Kim denied and had to stifle a chuckle at the mental image this conjured up. 'Why?'

'I thought if we went dancing it might be easier to get close to you without there being any misunderstandings with your dog.'

This time Kim didn't even try to stifle her laughter.

'It's not that funny,' he assured her.

'What exactly did you have in mind?'

'Sorry to fall into the category of your typical "businessmen" but I was wondering if you'd have dinner with me and then we could go on to a nightclub.'

'I am also sorry,' she said and directed a sparkling blue look up at him, 'for all the dangerous situations I've put you in, Mr Richardson. As for your suggestion, I like the sound of it very much and I will attempt to keep things safe for you.'

He grimaced.

'But I'll have to go home to get changed and then drive back into Bunbury—'

'I'll send a car for you,' he said, interrupting her.

Kim looked at him with a faint frown in her eyes as she wondered why he didn't pick her up himself.

He gestured. 'I have a heap of stuff to deal with—the penalty for taking a day off.'

'Well, OK. Thanks.'

'Seven-thirty suit you?' He raised an eyebrow at her.

'Fine, but really, I could drive in.'

'No.' He said it lightly but quite definitely.

'If that isn't an example of how you like to get your own way, I don't know what is,' she commented a little dryly.

'Not at all,' he denied. 'It's concern for your welfare, that's all.'

Several expressions chased across Kim's face, exasperation being foremost. Then her lips twisted and she looked rueful. 'Hoist by my own petard. All right.'

He laughed.

CHAPTER TWO

THERE was no one home when Kim got back to Saldanha from Margaret River.

There was nothing unusual in this. Her parents travelled frequently as well as socializing often and they were currently in Perth.

Kim taught at a boarding school down the coast at Esperance so she'd moved down there for term time but she spent the school holidays at home.

Fortunately, most of her formal clothes still resided in her bedroom at home and she was able to have a choice of what to wear for dinner and a nightclub with Reith Richardson.

Her bedroom was always a comfort to her. Her mother had given her carte blanche to redecorate it when she left school and she'd created a blue room, saying, 'If you can have a green room, why not a blue one?' And it was not only where she stored her clothes and slept, it was where she read, dreamed, played her harp and wondered sometimes what kind of a wife and mother she would be.

She showered and washed her hair while she thought

what she would wear, then, decision made, thought back over the day. And she was a little startled to feel a tremor run through her just at the thought of Reith Richardson…

I'm falling, she thought. In love or prey to a massive physical attraction? Strange, he didn't lay a hand on me today, other than just before… 'You made your intentions clear,' she said to Sunny Bob, who was lying on the carpet beside her.

The dog lifted his head and thumped his tail, then went back to sleep.

Kim grimaced and pictured what would have happened but for Sunny Bob. She would have revelled in Reith's arms, she knew. Just the thought of it now made her blush and she picked up her perfume bottle and touched the cool glass to her cheeks.

Whoa, she thought then. Take it slowly, Kim. Don't let this get out of hand. You need to know a lot more about this man…

She put the bottle down and picked up her brush, turning it slowly over and over in her hand as she thought of some of her actions today. Such as, for example, her precipitous dash from the cool and shade of the umbrella down the beach to the water earlier.

What had prompted that had been embarrassment. Yes, she wanted to know more about him but, in hindsight, asking him if he was married *had* sounded juvenile, and then intrusive, especially in the light of learning he had lost his wife.

So what was it about him that threw her off her usually even keel? she wondered. That underlying disapproval she'd sensed in him from the start? But why would he disapprove of her? Unless he thought she was completely wacky. But, if so, why would he want to keep on seeing her…?

Perhaps that was part of her enjoyment in his company, however—the light-hearted sparring she, at least, undertook, to challenge his perception of her?

She shook her head and stood up and got dressed. Her choice was a pair of dark grey palazzo pants and a silvery-grey halter top with wide lapels at the front and a low back. She wore no jewellery and no bra. Her shoes were high black sandals, her hair was sleek and smoothed back in a chignon.

Not over-dressed, not under-dressed, just right, she thought as she studied her reflection. The sun and the surf had given her a glow but there was still a frown in her eyes, indicating some inner unease.

She wandered over to her harp and plucked the strings. Romance, she conceded, had been a slightly bumpy road for her until she'd learnt to sort the wheat from the chaff—sort the men who were on the make and drawn by her wealthy parents and background more than by her soul, she thought with a dry little twist of her lips.

And, sadly, there had been more of the 'on the make' kind than the other with the result that she was very wary these days and on the lookout for fortune-hunters. Wary, somewhat hardened and definitely cynical. But did Reith Richardson fall into that class?

On the surface, it appeared not. He didn't seem to be at all interested in her background, but of course they'd only known each other for a short time. Yet there was something—her brow creased—a sort of stamp of authority about him that was impressive. There was also a reserve she sensed.

She sighed and picked up her purse at the sound of a car on the drive. 'Just—take it very slowly with this man,' she advised herself and went downstairs to be driven into town.

A few hours later, she stirred in his arms and said in a low husky voice, 'Do you ever take your own advice?'

He swung her round on the small, darkened, crowded floor with its coloured spotlights above, and they came together again. They'd danced for hours. It was the height of sophistication, the nightclub, on the second floor of a beautifully restored old building in Bunbury, and the music had been sensational.

'Sometimes.' He looked down at her rather wryly. 'How about you?'

'Not always.' She laid her head on his shoulder as, rather than dancing, they swayed to the music and, as she'd suspected, she revelled in being in his arms.

In fact, when she'd first laid eyes on him, when she'd walked into the restaurant and he'd stood up in a dark suit, the jacket of which had moulded his broad shoulders, she'd missed a step because he'd been so darkly attractive. From that moment on she'd been physically conscious of him in a way that had taken her by storm because she'd never felt this way before, never had her senses so stirred up by a man.

At the same time as a river of rhythm had flowed

through her veins, so had a river of sensuality. His hands on her hips had ignited a swathe of sensation up and down her body. And to rest her body against his, to feel the hard strength of him, the power, had made her feel as light as a feather and giddy with pleasure.

'Not always, which is very stupid of me. I—'

The music stopped, the band announced they were having a break and some recorded music took over.

Kim didn't finish what she was saying and sighed as they drew apart, then she led the way back to their table.

'More champagne?' he queried.

She shook her head. 'Just some iced water, thanks.'

'Not a bad idea,' he agreed. 'Why stupid? Now? At this moment in time?' he queried.

Kim put her elbows on the table and rested her chin on her clasped hands. 'I was going to take things very, very slowly with you, Mr Richardson,' she said. 'That was not supposed to include dancing the night away.' Kim smiled austerely. 'Do you have the same problem I have?'

He raised his eyebrows. 'The disinclination to keep my hands off you?'

'Something like that,' she said ruefully and thanked the waiter who brought them two glasses of iced water with slices of lemon. 'But perhaps we should—' She paused.

'We should look before we leap?' he suggested with some irony.

Kim narrowed her eyes as she caught the irony and said tartly, despite it being not what she wanted to do at all, 'My sentiments entirely.'

He put his head on one side and studied her. 'That annoyed you?'

'Not at all.'

'That I should feel we need to stop and think?' he persisted.

'Well…no, we should! But—' she paused '—you didn't sound entirely genuine. More, in fact, as if you were paraphrasing, with sarcasm, what you thought I would say.'

'It was the awful euphemism I used that offended me,' he said.

Kim stared at him. 'Look before we leap?' she murmured, then her lips curved and she started to laugh.

He put his hand over hers on the table and laughed with her, his dark eyes glinting with amusement.

Then he looked at his watch. 'Your car will be here shortly. I ordered it for midnight.'

Kim removed her hand. 'That solves that. I can go home feeling like Cinderella.'

He ignored that. 'Do you have any more time off?'

Kim blinked at the change of subject. 'Two more days.'

'Tomorrow, would you like to help me select some classy artwork?'

Her lips parted.

'You did say you had a good eye for art.'

'What's it for?'

'Some offices—some new offices in Perth. I'm not that keen on what the interior decorators have come up with.'

She thought for a moment then she shrugged. 'All

right. Yes, I'd like to. I have a couple of favourite galleries. You know—' she looked at him consideringly '—you're clever.'

He looked surprised. 'Why?'

'You've defused us. There we were, a pretty hot item on the dance floor, but now we're talking art and I'm about to be shipped off home.' She put her elbows on the table and rested her chin on her hands and narrowed her eyes. 'I'm just not sure why you're taking this course but you're right,' she said mischievously, 'you should *always* look before you leap.'

'Kim—' he pushed back his chair and stood up '—come with me.'

She raised her eyebrows but shrugged when she got no response and rose to follow him. He led her out of the main room, along a passage and onto a secluded balcony overlooking the street.

There Reith paused and looked up and down the street. Whatever he saw—nothing—must have gained his approval because he turned back to Kim, took her in his arms and kissed her swiftly but at the same time comprehensively.

So comprehensively she clutched him when their lips parted and she could only say his name on a note of stunned amazement as tremors of desire ran through her body.

'Kim?'

'You... I...I mean,' she stammered, 'why did you do that?'

His dark eyes rested on her lips, then the lovely line

of her throat and the curves of her breasts beneath the silvery-grey silk of her halter top.

'Why?' he repeated and smiled suddenly, a wicked little smile full of masculine arrogance. 'I wanted to.'

Kim gasped. 'That's… But I thought… *You* were the one who…hosed us down!'

He shrugged. 'You were the one who thought she was being shipped home like Cinderella.'

Kim touched her lips and opened her mouth to speak as a long black limousine pulled into the kerb down below.

She eyed it, then turned back to him. 'So?'

'I just wanted to make it clear that, while I believe we should exercise some caution, I'd much rather not be shipping you home.'

Kim stared up into his eyes and saw they were amused, wicked, but also just a shade rueful.

'You… You're serious,' she said incredulously.

'Uh-huh.'

'That…that makes me feel a bit better,' she conceded. 'OK—time and place for tomorrow?' she added huskily.

'You name it.'

She thought for a moment, then did so.

'Fine.' He bent his head and kissed her lightly. 'Goodnight. Sleep well.'

Kim donned black silk pyjamas and sat down at her dressing table when she arrived back at Saldanha.

'It's just you and me,' she murmured to Sunny Bob, who'd accorded her an enthusiastic but slightly puzzled welcome because of the strange black car.

'Puzzling days, you're right,' she said now as she smoothed cleanser onto her face and wiped it off with a tissue. 'For example, Sunny Bob,' she continued her conversation with the dog, 'I thought I felt better when he said he'd kissed me because he wanted to, and he wasn't that keen on shipping me home. Now I'm not so sure.'

She moistened a cotton pad with toner and patted it onto her skin, enjoying the cool feel of it.

Because the thing is—I do feel shipped home, she continued her monologue internally. What's more, I feel as if I'm the one making all the running, so to speak—how dare he do that to me?

Am I? she asked herself next, as she massaged a night cream into her skin. Making all the running?

No, look here, he keeps suggesting things, *he's* the one who keeps pushing us onwards and upwards.

She grimaced at her choice of words, then she thought, with a frown, yes, he does, but he's also the one who holds back. Why? Is there a sort of no-go zone around him or is it only my imagination? Why would that be, though, if it was so? Am I still a rather ridiculous little rich girl to him?

Am I being observed like some sort of scientific phenomenon he hasn't experienced before? Or is this stop/start approach meant to entice me on?

She put the tub of night cream with its gold top down with a little thump as a flash of annoyance at the thought claimed her, and she got up and roamed around the room.

Finally she got into bed and turned the light off but

her thoughts took another direction, one not greatly removed, however.

Should she call it off?

Should she pull a really arrogant, if not necessarily rich, stunt and simply not turn up tomorrow?

Or, even better, have a message delivered to him as he waited for her, to the effect that she'd decided she had better things to do…

She sat up suddenly as it struck her—forcibly—that it had only been two days—she'd only known Reith Richardson for two days! How could she be going through this level of turmoil for a man she barely knew?

She lay back and commanded herself to breathe slowly and calmly but it didn't work in helping her to fall asleep.

CHAPTER THREE

'SLEEP well?'

'No,' Kim said flatly.

'Neither did I, if it's any help,' Reith Richardson offered.

Kim switched her attention from the painting she was studying and looked up at him. She wore a fitted leather miniskirt in peach with a loose scarlet top in a filmy material. Her shoes were high cork wedges, her hair was looped back in a roll, she had big diamond-studded gold hoops in her ears and there were the faintest blue shadows beneath her eyes.

She looked, he thought wryly, gorgeous, from her red-gold hair down to those sensational legs, but moody. And he was presented with a sudden mental picture of her waking up in his bed with that same moody expression. Could she maintain it, though, if he cupped her breasts, then drew his hands down her body and made love to her slowly, very slowly, until they were both on fire? Careful, he warned himself, remember who this is…

She said, 'Why should it be any help?' then gestured as if to erase the words. 'It doesn't matter. Look, it's very difficult to choose art when you have no idea where it's going to end up.'

'I've got some sketches.'

'You've also got to be in the mood,' she added.

He paused and narrowed his eyes. 'I'm getting some pretty distressed vibes here so, starting at the top, is it that time of the month?'

'No,' she snapped.

'Is it the lack of really good sex then?' He shrugged. 'Can give you the blues.'

Kim beamed a glance of the opposite—pure blue fire—his way but at the same time a mental image of her lying naked in his arms and as aroused as he was streaked through her mind. And she couldn't for the life of her decide what annoyed her more—the tingle that went through her, lovely though it was, or the fact that he could do this to her after shipping her home last night.

'No,' she said through her teeth and was about to add a pithy comment, although she hadn't actually thought of one, but he interrupted.

'Have you had breakfast?'

She closed her mouth, then opened it again. 'What makes you think I didn't?' she answered.

'Did you?'

She looked mutinous. 'No.'

'Why not?'

She shrugged. 'I went for a ride, then I was running late.'

'Another wacky day in the making,' he commented, and put his arm through hers. 'Come.'

'Where? We haven't picked a thing yet.'

'You'll see.'

She shrugged again, as if to say she didn't give a damn one way or the other, and walked out with him.

An hour and a delicious mushroom omelette later, Kim looked around at the rustic restaurant he'd brought her to and said ruefully, 'You were right. Sorry. I feel much better.'

'Good. Is that all it was? A lack of food.'

'Don't start that again,' she warned, then grimaced as she recalled her turmoil of the night before. 'Not entirely, but I do find it hard to be miserable for long.'

'Miserable?' He frowned.

'Confused. Not one hundred per cent sure what game you're playing, Mr Richardson, put it that way.'

He raised an eyebrow and waited. When she offered no more, he said questioningly, 'Game?'

'I can't work out whether you're trying to seduce me or not.'

Their gazes clashed.

'There's a certain—' she moved her hands around each other '—stop/start approach you employ that I find a bit strange.'

'Are you suggesting we should jump into bed?'

Kim smiled but there was a touch of frost to it. 'No. But perhaps I should let you know that the disapproval and reserve is not all on your side.'

'That's what you think it is—disapproval?'

'Yes. Besides which, I have the feeling you're a loner at heart!' She said it almost jauntily.

'Would you prefer it if you had to fight me off?' he asked.

'Naturally not. Look, I've had enough of this conversation—you'll have me all gloom and doom again if we're not careful. Show me your sketches,' she commanded.

He pulled some papers out of his jacket pocket and handed them over to her.

She smoothed them out. 'Hmm…' she said eventually. 'Not bad. Do you have any preferences?' She opened her hands. 'Do you like your art conventional, for example, or could you live with a bit of—' she broke off and smiled suddenly '—wackiness?'

He stirred his coffee thoughtfully. 'I don't mind a bit of wackiness.'

'Good,' she approved briskly. 'Do you have any pet hates? For example, I don't like—sorry, I know you love it—but I don't like seascapes. With a passion.'

He looked amused. 'Why not?'

'I'm not sure. Perhaps you just can't capture the movement of the sea in paint. Any of those dislikes—or anything you particularly *like*?'

He rubbed his jaw. 'I've seen some Aboriginal art that has a sort of mysterious power that draws you in—it's hard to describe but it makes you feel it's alive.'

Kim put her cup down and sat up, her expression heavy with frustration. 'Why on earth didn't you tell me this sooner?'

'You have access to it?'

She nodded. 'I have friends who get right to the source, painters who still live in their traditional areas and are able to transfer the sheer magic—' she clenched a hand and her face glowed '—of their culture onto canvas.' She opened her purse and pulled out her phone. 'Hold thumbs they're not out in the desert.'

They weren't out in the desert so Kim took Reith to their gallery and they spent nearly the whole of the rest of the day going through canvases, making choices and deciding on frames.

Finally, he suggested dinner.

Kim agreed but told him she'd like to shower and change. 'And don't worry about sending me around in great big black limousines,' she told him. 'It doesn't do much for my mood. Anyway, I'm used to driving in and out of Bunbury.'

He looked at her, smiling. 'OK. What do you suggest restaurant-wise?'

She thought for a moment, then she told him with a toss of her head that she had a craving for pasta and nothing else would do. She also named a restaurant.

'So be it,' he said gravely.

Kim suffered a moment's disquiet. 'Do you like pasta? If you don't I suppose we could—'

'It would not be game to dislike pasta,' he broke in to say.

She looked disconcerted for a moment, then pulled a face at him and retreated to her car.

* * *

A couple of hours later, she parked her car in Bunbury and walked towards the restaurant.

She'd changed into a long, floaty flame-coloured dress streaked with white, and nude platform shoes. She'd left her hair loose and she carried a boxy little gold bag.

Reith was waiting for her and she walked towards him with her long free stride and her dress billowing around her, only to slow down then come to a stop a couple of feet away from him.

She shivered suddenly as his dark gaze roamed up and down her. Because there was something completely riveted about him and the way he was examining her body. In fact, she got the feeling she was naked beneath that compelling gaze, that he'd mentally undressed her, even dispensing with her underwear, and it was tense, yet, at the same time, incredibly erotic. It sent her pulses racing and tremors of desire running through her.

Then he moved and reached out to take her hand. 'You look sensational, Kim. Shall we go in?'

But she hesitated. 'You shouldn't do that to me. Not in public, Reith.'

'Sorry.' He didn't pretend to misunderstand. 'I couldn't help myself.'

She hesitated a moment longer.

He raised her hand and kissed her knuckles. 'I'm probably better off if I can see your legs,' he added.

Kim blinked, then said bewilderedly, 'The first time you saw them you nearly crashed!'

'Well, I could be over that now. But to be totally deprived makes me try to imagine them, you see.'

'Reith Richardson,' she said severely, 'you're talking utter claptrap. It's something men do all the time. Mind you—' she paused '—I have to confess you're pretty good at it.'

'Uh-huh?' He frowned. 'In what way?'

'When you get your face slapped, you'll know you're doing it wrong,' she advised. 'And now—may I eat? I'm starving!'

He laughed down at her and she turned a little pink because she knew he knew how affected she'd been by his mental undressing.

'I am starving,' she said a little lamely.

'All right. After you.'

'That turned out to be a much better day than I expected,' Kim said later. The Italian restaurant had candles in wine bottles and a folksy atmosphere and the pasta came highly recommended. 'Artwork-wise,' she added.

His lips twitched. 'You wouldn't be on commission, by any chance?'

She wrinkled her nose. 'No. But I wouldn't be surprised to get a bottle of French champagne and some Belgian chocolates for Christmas.' She smiled as a waiter poured her a glass of wine and she raised it in a toast to Reith. 'I hope you get a lot of pleasure out of your paintings, Mr Richardson!'

'Thank you, Miss Theron. Shall we order?'

She nodded, told him what she'd like and sat back. And they only spoke desultorily until their meals were served.

Then he said, 'Can we go back to our earlier discussion?'

'Which one was that?'

'The one,' he said, 'where you accused me of disapproving of you and failing to make my intentions clear.'

'Clear?'

He smiled dryly. 'Was I out to seduce you or not.'

'Oh, that one.' Kim sampled some fettuccine marinara, then raised a napkin to her lips. 'Mmm! OK. Are you?'

He narrowed his eyes. 'Would it be a problem?'

'Certainly,' Kim replied promptly.

'I might have thought otherwise last night on the dance floor.'

'Well, I might have too.' She gestured expansively. 'But that was last night. Today is a different matter.' Her eyes glinted very blue as she glanced at him then turned her attention back to her dinner.

'What about tomorrow?' he asked.

'I'm having a day off tomorrow.'

'I know, you told me. It's your last day off so—'

'What I mean is—' she interrupted '—I'm having a day off from *you*.'

He didn't miss a beat. He said, 'That's a pity, I was hoping you'd come to Clover Hill with me. I'm going over to look at some yearlings.'

Kim put her fork down. 'Horses?'

His lips twitched. 'So far as I know, that's all they breed at Clover.'

She clicked her tongue with some exasperation. 'I know that. Do you race horses?'

'Yes.'

'Is this an open day?'

He shook his head. 'A private viewing.'

Kim's eyes widened. 'You're getting a *private* viewing?'

He shrugged.

Kim simply stared at him. Clover Hill Stud was renowned throughout Australia in horse-breeding circles. Renowned for the stallions they stood and the percentage of winners amongst their progeny. It was also a showplace with a beautiful old homestead, magnificent gardens and paddocks. And if Reith Richardson had gone out of his way to pick an outing Kim Theron would not be able to resist he couldn't have chosen better. But, of course, he couldn't have gone out of his way; this would probably have been arranged well beforehand...

'Kim?'

She blinked, then shook her head. 'I don't know how you do it but you're a master tactician. Thank you, I cannot tell a lie, I've never been to Clover Hill and I would love to see it.'

'You obviously know a bit about horses.' It was a statement rather than a question.

'I know a bit,' Kim agreed. 'I've ridden since I was six and my parents raced them. But, hang on, Penny is going home tomorrow—not that she needs me, her mum and hubby are both here now—but I'd like to spend a couple of hours with her when she gets back. So I'll probably be tied up until after lunch.'

He sat back and pushed his plate away. 'You take good care of your friends, don't you?'

She lifted her shoulders. 'Who doesn't? So—'

'It's not a problem if you could meet me there at two o'clock.'

Kim smiled with noticeable radiance. 'Done!'

Her parents were home but in bed when she got back that night.

She took care not to wake them but was surprised when her father stayed in bed the next morning.

'He's not feeling well,' her mother confided, closing his bedroom door—they had separate bedrooms.

'Has he seen a doctor?'

'No.' Fiona Theron tightened the sash of her beautiful silk dressing gown. 'But I'll keep an eye on him. So, what have you been doing with yourself, darling?' She led the way downstairs to the breakfast room.

'This and that,' Kim heard herself say and grimaced as she thought how evasive the phrase had sounded to her when uttered by Reith Richardson. So she made an effort to elaborate but something kept her from mentioning Reith and she waxed lyrical instead on the subject of Penny's baby.

The housekeeper, Mary Hiddens, came in with a coffee pot.

'Hi, Mary! How's the family?' Kim enquired as she helped herself to some bacon and French toast from a silver warmer, and poured herself a cup of coffee.

'All well, thank you, Kim,' Mary replied, then turned to Fiona, who had taken nothing from the warmer but reached now for the coffee pot.

'Ma'am, please have some breakfast,' Mary said.

'Just now, Mary. You know how I always have to whet my whistle first!'

Mary hesitated, then withdrew and Kim looked at her mother curiously. 'You're not dieting, are you, Mum? You don't need to; you look marvellous!' She studied her mother's slim waistline.

'No, no,' Fiona said hastily. 'So you're back to Esperance tomorrow?'

'Uh-huh.' Kim fed some bacon to Sunny Bob, who placed his head lovingly in her lap. 'But it's not that long to the school holidays, then I'll be home for a month.'

'Lovely,' Fiona said, but with a curious lack of conviction.

Kim frowned and opened her mouth, but her father could be heard calling for her mother.

'Do you want me to call the doctor, Mum?' she asked.

'No. No,' her mother repeated with her hand on the door handle. 'He'll be fine. Have a nice day, sweetheart!'

Clover Hill exceeded Kim's expectations.

The rose gardens alone were worth the visit but she loved the parade of yearlings, still flighty, still to partake in their first official yearling sale, still, some of them, with short bushy tails and frizzy manes.

The stud-master sat with them on a stand in the parade ring and gave them a run-down on the horses' breeding as the little ones pranced around the ring.

'Will you buy today?' Kim asked Reith.

He shook his head. 'Some of them are barely broken in to lead, some aren't, but it's interesting to be able to keep track of them from an earlier age, before they hit the sales ring.'

'Do you have your own trainer?'

'No. I spread them around: Perth, Melbourne, Sydney.'

Kim frowned. 'How many horses do you have in training?'

He rubbed his jaw. 'About twenty.'

Kim swallowed. She had a very good idea how much that would cost. 'Many winners?'

'Not yet.' He looked down at her amusedly. 'Haven't been in the game that long.'

'Rescuing businesses in trouble must be profitable,' she commented.

He said nothing and they walked in silence for a while. They were on their own now; the stud-master had left them after inviting them to have a wander around.

It was a cool, overcast day, unusual for the time of year. Kim wore jeans, boots and a navy leather bomber jacket, whereas Reith had a lined anorak over his shirt and jeans and suede desert boots.

Kim remembered him handling the horses when they'd visited the foals still with their mums in the paddock. It was obvious he knew his horses—a man after my own heart, she thought with a fleeting smile.

Now, as they strolled along a swept path, a sharp little breeze got up and she moved closer to him.

'Feels as if it's come up from the Antarctic, that breeze,' she said with a shiver.

He put an arm around her and drew her towards a creeper-covered shelter with a bench inside. Inside, as they sank down onto the bench, they found themselves protected from the breeze but he pulled her closer.

She breathed deeply and nestled against him but at the same time she had no idea what was coming next between them.

'So, back to work tomorrow,' he murmured.

'Mmm...'

'Looking forward to it?'

Kim hesitated and, rather than answering, asked a question herself. 'What will you be doing?'

'I'm off to points north for a few weeks.'

A little of the Antarctic chill seemed to enter her soul, let in, she thought, by the casualness of his words but, not only that, by the lack of detail.

The thought transferred to a larger issue between them—the lack of *all* she knew about him. And refused to ask now, yes, she acknowledged, despite how close she felt to him. She couldn't think of anywhere she'd rather be than sitting close to him, breathing in his essence, conscious of his bulk and strength, but there was a huge mental divide between them.

She moistened her lips and asked another question. 'Reith, how did we come to this?'

'You don't think we should have come to "this"?' he queried.

'I'm just a bit surprised, but that's not what I meant,' Kim confessed. 'To begin with I saw us more as adversaries...well, maybe not that so much, but enjoying fencing, verbally, with each other. Now—'

'You tend to forget—' he interrupted '—that one glimpse of your legs nearly drove me into a tree.'

Kim laughed softly. 'You were furious with me at the time, though,' she reminded him and deepened her voice. *'Lady—are you mad?'*

He grimaced.

'But this is what I still don't know—are you trying to seduce me or not?' She leant her head on his shoulder.

He loosened one hand and slipped some strands of her hair under her cheek. 'I can't tell a lie,' he conceded. 'Well, the thought of going to bed with you, Kimberley Theron, is, paradoxically, keeping me awake at night.'

She moved her cheek on the fabric of his jacket. 'I must say I've also thought about it.' She looked up into his eyes. 'You must know that. Not—' she pulled herself out of his arms and sat up '—that I'm going to do it.'

His lips twisted and he looked down at her quizzically. 'No?'

She shook her head. 'Not yet, anyway.'

'Does that mean to say I'm on a promise?'

She chuckled and leant back against him, growing serious. 'What I mean is, I think we need to know each other better.' She paused. And suddenly realized that she meant it. This uncertainty about what he felt for her and vice versa—about what would become of them—had become like an emotional roller coaster for her and she had to find a way to get off.

'What would you like me to know about you?' he queried.

'I would like,' she said somewhat darkly, 'not to be classified as a spoilt socialite, a ditsy redhead or—at least you can't accuse me of being a dumb blonde—'

He interrupted her by the simple expedient of putting a finger to her lips. Then he bent his head and started to kiss her.

Kim was lost. Lost beneath the finesse of his touch as he cupped her face and his fingers slid down the side of her neck, causing her to shiver in delight and anticipation.

'You do that so well,' she whispered when their lips parted.

'Thank you,' he murmured, but added, 'You expected me to do it like the local yokel or a country hick, Miss Theron?'

She wrinkled her nose. 'Not at all. I just didn't expect you to do it better than anyone else I've ever known.'

He lifted his head and looked down at her with a glimmer of humour in his dark eyes. 'Either you haven't been kissed a lot or—' He stopped.

'Or what? I've made lousy choices in men?'

'You said it,' he returned ruefully.

'You thought it.' Kim leant back against him. 'But it could be true. I'd hate to think what you could do to me if you really tried. But—' she hesitated as some sanity returned and she recalled her conviction that she had to get off the roundabout '—Reith, we don't need to rush into anything, do we?'

She felt him move against her.

She took a breath. 'Do we?' she queried, at the same time conscious of an alarm bell going off inside her.

He hesitated. 'Has something gone wrong?'

'No.' As she said it, it occurred to her that it wasn't quite true but how to explain her reservations accurately? Or should she lighten up a bit until she could be more articulate?

'Tell me a bit more about you, though. Where do you actually live, for example?' she asked teasingly.

He laughed. 'I spend so much time on the move it's hard to say. But I have an apartment in Perth where my offices are and it's where Darcy comes home to for the school holidays.'

'Darcy,' Kim said on an unexpected breath. 'So… he's at boarding school? But he's only ten.'

'And he's not the only ten-year-old boarder.'

'True,' Kim conceded slowly, 'although we have very few that young in the school where I teach.'

'He's only been there for six months since his grandmother died.'

'Your wife's mother?'

He nodded. 'She more or less brought him up. But he seems to have settled down well.'

'I hope you spend a lot of time with him,' Kim said severely.

'As much as I can.'

'Talking of time,' she added, 'I need to spend a bit of time at home.' She frowned as it occurred to her that something had felt different about 'home' lately but she hadn't been able to put her finger on it.

'You don't live at home?'

'For the last year I've been living in Esperance, that's where I teach, so I've been out of the home "loop", so to speak,' she said slowly, then shrugged. 'But it's school holidays in a week or so.'

He paused, then picked up her hand. 'I can't visualize you as a teacher.'

'Neither could I, at first.' She shrugged. 'Then I found I had a knack for it. I really like kids.'

'I thought something entrepreneurial would be more in your line.'

'Oh, a friend and I have opened a gallery in Esperance. Not paintings but metalwork, pottery, papier mâché, really creative knitting, et cetera.' Her eyes glinted. 'Satisfied?'

He took her chin in his hand and dropped a light kiss on her lips. 'Yes.' Then he looked narrowly into her eyes. 'We're not parting on bad terms, are we?'

She looked up at him, completely sober now, and knew that this man, this mystery man, could be the one to lure her onto the rocks. The rocks of loving him without being loved in return.

She had no idea how she knew this; it was an instinct that somehow told her he was a loner… Yes, there was no doubt he was quite cagey about his life—for that matter, so was she. Apart from one mention of Saldanha, she'd told him nothing about her family, nothing about Balthazar.

Come to that, she thought with a blink, he hadn't asked her a single question about her background.

She grimaced and returned to this loner she sensed in him, this *something* that told her he maintained an emotional exclusion zone around him…

And yet they were always good together; they seemed to have a rapport, a similar sense of humour, a similar sense of what was fine, even a similar taste in music. And now it even seemed as if he could read her mind. As if he could sense her uncertainty beneath her attempts to make light of it. So *where* did this feeling come from?

'Kim?'

She came back from her thoughts. 'No. Not on bad terms. Guess what?'

He looked at her.

'Penny's settled on a name for their baby. Reith.'

His eyebrows shot up. 'Because I gave you a lift?'

'No. Because it's unusual and she likes it. When are you going?'

'Tomorrow afternoon.'

'Then I won't see you until you come back.'

He grimaced but said, 'I'll look forward to it. Kim?'

'No, Reith,' she said quietly. 'That's how we should leave it.'

'Or…like this.' He gathered her in his arms and kissed her deeply.

Then he surprised her. He rubbed his chin on the top of her head and said, 'What do you think of this place?'

'Clover Hill?' She looked around the paddocks and their horses, at the roses and the creeper-covered homestead, at the Darling Hills in the background, and she breathed deeply and smiled. 'It's special. Why?'

He shrugged. 'Just asking. OK, time to go.'

But after he'd watched her drive off, Reith didn't leave immediately. He leant back against the car and attempted to think things through.

Such as being accused of a stop/start approach in his attempts to seduce Kimberley Theron.

He shoved his hands in his pockets and chewed his lip. She was right, of course. Every now and then his conscience pricked him. And every now and then he felt guilt associated with Sylvia, his wife, the guilt he'd felt at wanting her but not being able to love her. As for Kim, he'd even once asked himself why he hadn't rung for roadside assistance for her that first day and simply driven off when he well knew her family would hate him having anything to do with her.

For that matter, why hadn't he just told her? He'd been on the brink of it several times. But, despite his growing respect for her, he knew well enough that that could lose her to him. The more you got to know Kim Theron, the more evidence there was that loyalty to friends was paramount with her. It made sense that loyalty to her family would be the same. But she was no fool, so…?

He left the question hanging in the air, but one thing he did know was that he wasn't prepared to lose her.

Not yet.

He grimaced and got into his car. But, instead of driving away from Clover Hill, he drove from the stables round to the house…

Two weeks later, Kim made a discovery that horrified her.

She'd been preoccupied since her parting from Reith. Up in the air and down in the dumps described her alternating state of mind accurately. Would she ever see him again? Why did life seem dull and sepia because he wasn't around? Could you fall deeply in love in four days?

Should she have got some contact details at least, instead of allowing her mobile number to be the only link between them? Although he did know where to find her.

Then school had broken up and she'd come home for the holidays. A couple of days later, she came home one evening to find her father slumped on the floor in the lounge, apparently unconscious.

She checked his pulse and flew upstairs to get her mother, gabbling at the same time about how he must have tripped on the rug or…

'No, darling, he's drunk,' Fiona Theron said sadly as she twisted her thin hands and stared down at her comatose husband.

'Drunk?' Kim echoed incredulously.

Fiona nodded. 'It happens a lot these days.'

'Why?'

'We're going under, sweetheart. I begged him to tell you but he keeps…well…hoping for a miracle.'

'I don't believe this,' Kim whispered. 'Why didn't Damien tell me?' Damien was her older brother and her father's second in command.

'Damien…' Fiona gestured helplessly. 'But anyway…'

'No! Tell me about Damien,' Kim insisted.

'Damien—' her mother swallowed painfully '—oh, look, Damien is not a businessman, Kim. You must know that. Horses are his life.' Fiona paused and burst into tears.

* * *

The next morning at ten, Kim held an emergency family meeting. She looked so pale, and still so confused, her father and brother, both of whom would have preferred to be a million miles away, thought twice about it and attended.

'Tell me, Dad,' she begged. 'Tell me what's happened.'

Frank Theron was a big man, silver-haired now but still good-looking, although he had a livid bruise on his cheek from his collapse last night, and other signs Kim hadn't noticed that all was not well—red veins in his cheeks, prominent pouches beneath his eyes.

'Kim,' he said on a heavy sigh, 'the last five years have been very difficult. We've had several outbreaks of powdery mildew and you know how that can affect not only the grapes but wine quality. We've had a drought, then floods, then a fire. We've had a global financial downturn.' He stopped to sigh again. 'And we live quite an extravagant lifestyle.'

Damien, her brother, looked down. He maintained a stable of polo ponies. Kim looked at the lovely designer dress she wore and thought of her sports car, her twenty-first birthday present…

'So?' she queried.

'So we put the winery on the market,' Frank continued, looking animated for the first time, although angrily so, 'and attracted the attention of a complete upstart!'

'I wouldn't call him that,' Fiona murmured.

'You mightn't but I would,' her husband insisted.

'What does he know about wine, about grapes? He was born in a boundary rider's hut on some godforsaken cattle station. And he had the nerve to offer me a pittance. For Balthazar!'

'Upstart or not,' Damien Theron said moodily, 'he's made a fortune.' Damien had inherited their mother's dark eyes and hair and their father's height but not his bulk. He was whip-thin but that was deceptive—when you saw him on a headstrong horse, you couldn't doubt he was strong. 'You have to admit that, Dad,' he added.

Frank turned angrily on his son but Kim intervened.

'Just a minute. If he was born in a boundary rider's hut, how can he be offering… Even a pittance for Balthazar has got to be quite a sum!'

'Mining,' Frank said succinctly. 'He bought a mine no one else wanted and the rest—i.e., a fortune when he sold it—is history. Now he specializes in buying rundown companies. He waits until they're on their knees, then comes in like a scavenger.'

Kim's lips parted and a shiver ran down her spine as a dreadful premonition took her in its grip…

'What's his name?' she asked with a dry throat.

Her father waved a hand. 'Doesn't matter. Don't concern yourself, Kimmie.'

'I must.' She swivelled her gaze to her brother. 'S-so…so you rejected his offer?' Her voice shook.

Damien sighed and nodded. 'Not only that, he's bought Clover Hill. I heard the news yesterday. I don't suppose he'll be interested in another property in the same area.'

Kim dropped the papers she was holding. 'Bought Clover Hill?' she whispered. 'What's his *name*?'

'Richardson,' her father answered shortly.

'Reith Richardson,' Fiona contributed. 'Rather unusual… Kim, dear, you look dreadful. Is there anything the matter? Anything else, I mean?'

CHAPTER FOUR

IT WAS two weeks after she'd learnt the true state of affairs at home before Kim saw Reith again.

Which turned out to be plenty of time to find herself in even greater turmoil than she'd been in before he'd taken off for 'points north'.

She couldn't forgive herself for not sensing that things were badly wrong at home a lot sooner than she had. It made her flinch to think that Mary, the housekeeper, had been concerned for her mother, who was eating poorly, whereas she herself had not even noticed it.

It hurt her to think she'd not interpreted her father's pent-up rage correctly or even taken much notice of it. And she could have kicked herself for not realizing Damien's heart wasn't in the winery. True, she and Damien had never been that close—there were five years between them—but all the same…

Then Reith rang and suggested dinner.

She suggested lunch instead.

They met at a country pub, also her suggestion, not far from Saldanha. She drove there in an estate station wagon; she'd sold her convertible. The money had been like a drop in the ocean but it had made her feel she was contributing something to the mountain of debt facing the family.

She walked into the pub, wearing jeans and a check shirt and with her hair fish-plaited. Her heart banged once at the sight of him, also in jeans and a black T-shirt, but she ignored it and pulled out a chair…

'Kim.' He stood up and studied her closely. Somehow the dimensions of her face were different, the changes wrought by stress, blue shadows beneath her eyes, but the whole beautiful although in a new way, and he went still. 'You know,' he said then.

She sat down. 'I know,' she repeated. 'When, as a matter of interest, were you thinking of telling me?'

'Today,' he said laconically and signalled to the barman, who brought over a bottle of wine and poured her a glass. Reith had a tankard of beer. The pub, adorned with ancient saddles, bridles and other horse memorabilia, was empty apart from them.

'Oh, that's easy enough to say, Reith,' she taunted.

'It's true.'

She stared at him with her lips working, then took a sip of wine to steady herself. 'Why? Why didn't you tell me who you were?'

He sat back and rested his arm along the back of the chair beside him. 'I…' He paused and narrowed his eyes. 'Did it matter if you knew who I was or not?'

'Of course it did! My father regards you as public enemy number one. He feels you've offered him a pittance for Balthazar, but not only that, you don't have the…the expertise to do justice to what is a famous name.' She stopped, frustrated. Because, at the back of her mind, although she was employing her father's arguments, she wasn't a hundred per cent convinced they were correct. 'Look,' she said, 'my father—'

'Thinks I'm an upstart from beyond the black stump? It's OK, I know; he told me,' Reith drawled. 'As for your brother, with his polo ponies and his old school tie—we might as well be on different planets.' He paused and narrowed his eyes. 'I was hoping you mightn't share their opinion.'

'Were you? Were you really, Reith? This is my family we're talking about. This isn't just a winery and an estate, not to me it isn't. It's something that goes way back…'

'Look, Kim—' he broke in '—that's all very well but sentiment is no match for cold hard facts. It doesn't pay the bills.'

She glared at him, then closed her eyes briefly. 'Perhaps you're right,' she said tonelessly. 'But perhaps,' she added with more fire, 'you could never understand how we feel unless you've been in a similar position. Not only that, I always suspected you were impossible to get through to.'

He frowned. 'What do you mean?'

She paused, then said, 'That there's an exclusion zone around you I would never have got through on a personal level and this is just an extension of that.'

Their gazes clashed.

'Did it not matter one way or another who I was?' she asked and her eyes widened. 'Or was it precisely because I was a Theron, a member of a family you had cause to despise, that you…that you… Oh! Of course!' She blinked. 'That explains it. Why I got the distinct impression you didn't approve of me even while you were…you were…' She stopped breathlessly but her eyes were accusing.

There was a brittle little pause, then he said dryly, 'How we came to meet was due to a wacky episode of *your* making, Kim. I would never have sought you out. Come to that, if I could have got out of giving you that lift I would have, but did you honestly expect me to leave you there?'

'You didn't have to ask me to dinner,' she reminded him bitterly.

He looked away as a party of men in khaki clothes and boots came in and threw their dusty hats down.

He looked back at last. 'Well, you see, Kim, by then I was wondering what it would be like to make love to you. Whether, like the rest of your family, you'd be an arrogant Theron—even in bed.'

She gasped. She did more. She picked up her wine glass to dash the contents in his face but he caught her wrist and held it in an iron grip until she was forced to put the glass down.

'No violence, Kim,' he warned softly.

She subsided and he released her wrist. But he could see the blue fire in her eyes and the *hauteur* in the set of her mouth, both clear indications that he was now persona non grata in her estimation, and he discovered he had a devil riding in him with regard to Kimberley Theron.

He still wanted her. In fact he wanted her more than ever…

He was also reminded of something he'd said to his secretary on the subject of Francis Theron's apparently stunning daughter—*maybe they need to find her a rich husband…* How ironic, he thought to himself.

'Besides, I've got a proposition to put to you,' he said to her.

'Obviously not a business one,' she retorted.

He shrugged. 'You could say so.'

Her eyes widened. 'But I thought you'd withdrawn your offer. I believe you've bought Clover Hill instead!' Her eyes challenged him. 'Something else you didn't see fit to tell me.'

He grimaced. 'I hadn't entirely made up my mind then but, yes, I did buy Clover Hill.'

'So?' she queried impatiently.

He took his time and allowed his dark gaze to roam over her. 'Marry me,' he said slowly. 'If you do, I'll save your parents from bankruptcy.'

Three weeks later, they stood side by side at a register office and were pronounced man and wife.

Kimberley Maria Richardson née Theron wore a filmy dress splashed with oversized blooms in cream and rose-pink on a pale grey background. The dress had a blouson bodice with a dropped waistline and a three-quarter skirt and carried a very famous designer label. It lived up to its label in every way so she looked marvellous, although she was a little pale.

Reith Richardson—no middle name, Kim thought; is

that significant?—then chastised herself for being ridiculous, but the fact of the matter was her mind was turning crazy circles. It had been since the day she'd agreed to marry Reith because she couldn't bear to think of her parents ending up in the poor house, so to speak.

They had no one to witness their union so the magistrate obliged, then they were seated side by side in his car and speeding towards Saldanha for the next momentous encounter—breaking the news to her parents.

She'd insisted on doing things this way, although now she was beginning to regret the decision. Beginning to regret not taking his offer to break the news himself.

'What can *you* say?' she'd taunted. 'In exchange for your daughter I'll get you out of hock?'

'No,' he'd replied. 'I could say that an intense attraction has sprung up between us and—'

She'd turned on him. 'Believe me, it's died an instant death!'

He'd watched her impassively for a long moment then he'd shot her last hopes down in flames. 'Kim, I don't know about you but the alternative for your parents would be disastrous. Both Balthazar and Saldanha would go into receivership. This way, my offer for them will clear the debts, your father'll have a place on the Balthazar board in an advisory capacity and *you* will get to play lady of the manor at Saldanha.' His eyes had mocked her.

She'd gone white. 'If you think insulting me is going to help, you're wrong. Why can't Mum and Dad stay on at Saldanha?'

'It would never work.'

'I don't think they've got anywhere else to go,' she'd objected. Then she'd bitten her lip and said painfully, 'They may be able to clear their debts if they sell to you but I don't think there'll be anything left over.' She'd pressed her hands into fists at the thought of the absolute mess she'd found her parents' personal finances to be in; at the thought of them honourably solvent rather than bankrupted, but only just, only a hair's breadth from being out on the street.

He'd noticed the gesture. 'Your brother,' he'd suggested.

Kim had shaken her head. 'Damien has no more resources than I have.'

She'd taken a deep breath then and risked saying, 'I don't think you're rating me highly enough, Reith, to be honest.'

'Oh?' He'd raised an eyebrow.

'No. As a wife, especially for a billionaire, I'll be superb.'

They'd stared at each other and it became a prickly-tense, heart-stopping moment.

'Do you mean in bed?' he'd queried at last, with a significant scan up and down her figure that effectively stripped her naked but not in a humorous way at all.

'Now, that,' she'd said, inwardly threatening to shoot herself if she blushed but in fact she was way too angry to blush, 'might depend on you so I'll suspend judgement until it happens...*if* it happens. What I meant was that I would run your homes beautifully, I'd handle the entertaining a billionaire might find appropriate with ease, I'd look the part and—' she'd paused '—I'm good with kids.'

Reith had said slowly, 'I've got an apartment in Bunbury; I'll lease it to your parents rent-free and I'll set up an allowance for them—for as long as you stay with me, Kim.'

She'd drawn a breath. 'You drive a hard bargain.'

'You're not exactly playing softball yourself,' he'd said derisively.

She'd opened her mouth to protest that it was no such thing but said instead, 'Why shouldn't it be a game two can play?'

'Indeed. Why not?' he'd responded with a flash of humour that had infuriated her. She hadn't been mollified when he'd added, 'But you certainly deserve full marks for standing behind your nearest and dearest, Kim Theron.'

Now, as the miles got chewed up, as the roads became country ones and they got closer, she became less and less certain she was doing this the right way round. Less certain that she shouldn't have warned her parents first…

'Stop,' she said suddenly. 'Please stop. I feel sick.'

He pulled up on the side of the road. There was a fairly broad grassy verge, then a fence and a line of bushes beyond, indicating a water course of some kind.

Kim swallowed frantically several times, then pushed her door open precipitously and stumbled out, and there followed a painful little interlude for her, during which she lost what little she'd eaten that day.

Eventually she staggered back to the car and sat down on the seat sideways.

'Here.'

She squinted upwards to see Reith minus his suit jacket and with his tie loosened and his shirtsleeves pushed up, offering her a wet towel.

'Where… How?' she stammered.

'The towel's been in the back since we went surfing. And—' he gestured behind him '—there's a creek over the fence. The water is flowing and clean.'

'Oh, thank you.' She took the towel gratefully and held it to her face and neck. 'Sorry but—'

'Don't be,' he said, interrupting her, and took the towel from her. 'I'll wet it again. There's also a bottle of drinking water in the console.' He leant past her and pushed a button, revealing a plastic bottle of spring water.

Half an hour later they were on their way again.

Reith had tossed his jacket in the back seat and Kim had done what she could to restore herself.

'Don't worry about it,' he advised after glancing at her. They were proceeding, she noticed, at a much slower pace. 'You look fine,' he said. He added very quietly, 'You always do.'

She turned her head to look at him and their gazes clashed briefly before she looked away.

What does that *mean*? she wondered.

Should I be complimented? Complimented enough to forgive him for forcing me to marry him? Does he honestly think that's all it's going to take? Still, he was kind just now, and helpful—if *only* I knew exactly what I was dealing with.

'What are you going to say to your parents, Kim?'

She tensed as his question broke the silence, and pleated the silk chiffon of her skirt. 'I don't know.'

'That doesn't sound particularly like you,' he observed with a tinge of sarcasm.

She bridled but forced herself to simmer down. 'I was just going to…to present it as a fait accompli, but I don't think that's going to work, now that I come to think of it,' she said. Then she took a breath. 'Perhaps,' she said slowly, 'what you had in mind to say is…the best way to go.'

'At least it's honest.'

'No, it's not honest, Reith, from the point of view of getting married because of it but—' she hesitated '—all right; I'll go along with it.'

'We don't have to make such heavy weather of this, Kim. Not that long ago, we were good together,' he said as he changed gear and swung into Saldanha's driveway.

She took a very deep breath. 'You're right,' she agreed, and took some more deep breaths as she prepared to face her parents.

In the event, however, the encounter proved to be catastrophic.

Kim groaned as they pulled under the rear portico. 'Damien's here.' She pointed towards the parked racing-green sports car. She frowned.

'We might as well get it all over and done with.' Reith switched the engine off and got out of the car.

He retrieved his jacket from the back seat, fixed his shirtsleeves, fiddled with his tie and came round to open her door.

Kim didn't move for a moment as she stared down at the shiny gold band now on the ring finger of her left hand—she'd refused an engagement ring. As she did so, she thought of her parents, thought of all they'd done for her, and she found the strength to slip out of the car without his assistance.

But what greeted them as she led the way inside, stopping only to pat a delighted Sunny Bob, was a scene of trauma. Her father was slumped on the settee in the main lounge, her mother was kneeling beside him crying. Mary Hiddens was hovering, wringing her hands, and Damien was savagely punching numbers into his phone.

'Kim…Kim…' Her mother caught sight of her. 'Oh, Kim!' Her gaze fell on Reith and she gasped. 'So it's true!'

'What's true?' Kim ran forward to kneel down beside her mother.

'Some journalist just rang your father and asked him if it was true that you'd married Reith Richardson. He hadn't been feeling well, your father, but that…at that… he just collapsed.'

'You've probably killed him,' Damien said darkly to Reith.

Thanks to Reith's best efforts—he'd taken command—Frank survived the attack.

Reith had told Damien not to worry about calling an

ambulance and instead he'd summoned a medical emergency helicopter. He'd made Frank as comfortable as possible until it had arrived, and administered some of the emergency medicine Frank had been prescribed but no one had thought to give him in their panic.

And he'd been with Kim when the specialist told her that her father had a heart condition that had been ticking away like a time bomb, a condition that might or might not respond to open-heart bypass surgery—something her father dreaded.

The specialist had also told her that the attack could have happened at any time.

'How did anyone find out? About us?'

She asked the question in a vague, distracted way when they were alone at Saldanha. Her mother had been persuaded to be admitted to the hospital and sedated, Damien was still at the hospital and arrangements were being made for bypass surgery on Frank as soon as possible. The subject of her marriage to Reith Richardson had apparently sunk from sight beneath the weight of the medical emergency, for both Damien and her mother.

Once again, Reith had discarded his jacket and loosened his tie. He'd poured them both a brandy.

'Someone must have recognized—you, most probably. Kim—' he paused '—what do you want to do?'

She sipped some brandy and laid her head back. 'What do you mean? Now? In a week's time? When?'

'Now, for starters,' he said dryly.

'Look, I don't know,' she replied frustratedly. 'I can't

think straight.' She looked around the lovely room with a frown and it occurred to her that Reith looked, if not exactly at home, almost as if he knew his way around it.

But, of course, she thought then, he's been here before, hasn't he? My father or Damien probably offered him a drink out of the cocktail cabinet, so that was how he knew where to find the brandy. Of course they wouldn't have been offering him drinks after he made his first paltry offer for Balthazar… She paused her thoughts.

'Tell me something,' she said with another frown. 'Were Saldanha and Balthazar just business propositions to you? Not any desire to live here and be involved in the wine industry or…' She trailed off, then gathered steam again. 'Or put down roots that have more substance than the boundary rider's hut on some godforsaken cattle station—' She stopped abruptly and put a horrified hand to her mouth.

He watched her for a long moment, narrowly, but otherwise curiously without expression. Then he said, 'It wasn't a boundary rider's hut—but I suppose you could call it a godforsaken cattle station. It was out from Karratha.' He grimaced. 'No, in answer to your question. I'm not interested in roots or substance, so I'm never going to appeal to your father or brother, Kim. I'm never going to be good enough for you in their estimation. If that's what you're wondering.'

Kim sat up abruptly. 'Why *do* they… Why are they *so* against you, though, Reith?'

He rolled his balloon glass between his hands and

stared down at the cognac. 'They consider me a country hick who had a bit of luck with a patch of dirt.'

'But you're not a country hick. I mean—'

'You mean I don't uncap beer bottles with my teeth? No, I don't. I do lack an old school tie, though.'

'That's rubbish.'

He shrugged.

'There's got to be more to it,' Kim persisted, although she wasn't sure why. It was just that she was so tired, so shocked by the events of the day, yet this was the one topic her mind seemed to want to pursue, as if it had an extraordinary significance.

Reith took a long sip of his brandy, then put the glass down and pushed it away from him. 'It's probably because I was able to expose all the mistakes they made over the past few years, the misjudgements—'

'But I thought it was flood, fire, drought, global financial crises—' she interrupted '—powdery mildew! And so on. Things you couldn't prevent, in other words.'

'They didn't help, but there were no contingency plans in place, for one thing. Kim, look—' he rubbed his jaw '—it's how I operate. It's by digging beneath the surface that I can accurately evaluate what I'm getting into, but it doesn't necessarily endear me to the people on the other end of it.'

He got up abruptly and came to stand in front of her with his hands shoved into his pockets. 'Look,' he said, 'I'm sorry about your father but, little though he knows it, you'll be better off with me than—'

'How can you *say* that?' Kim stumbled to her feet.

'You make me feel like a…a commodity! And there's no way you can know what my welfare depends on.'

'Kim, I know exactly what ensures your welfare. I only have to kiss you to—'

She raised her hand to slap him but he caught her wrist and pulled her into his arms.

'Don't,' he warned softly.

'Let me go,' she said through her teeth.

'No. Not until we've sorted something out.'

'Well, sort away!' she commanded. 'Just don't you dare kiss me.' But, despite the command, tears ran down her cheeks.

He grinned fleetingly. 'That's more like the girl I know. No, listen.' He tightened his grip on her as she wriggled. 'I'm not expecting you to leap into the marital bed in these circumstances—' he gestured '—your father, I mean—unless you'd like to?'

Kim refused to look at him but he didn't let her go. 'Take that as a definite no, Richardson,' he murmured to himself. 'Then it'll have to be a moratorium.'

Kim stilled and turned towards him. 'What do you mean?'

He lifted a sardonic eyebrow. 'A freeze on all contentious matters. For a period of time.'

'Why don't we just separate and get a divorce?'

'No, Kim.'

She stared up at him. 'Just—no, Kim?'

'Uh-huh.'

She sagged against him. 'I can't believe this,' she said, distraught.

'Life does hand out some brickbats,' he agreed.

She opened her mouth on a sharp retort, then closed it, nearly biting her tongue in the process because, of course, it was true.

'But for the time being,' he went on, 'while your father is so sick, we won't make any lifestyle decisions or major changes.'

Kim straightened and looked into his eyes. 'Where will you stay? Bunbury? Perth?'

He shook his head. 'Clover Hill.'

She gasped. 'Have you taken possession?' But she immediately fired another question. 'What's wrong with Clover—what did you have to ferret out about it before you bought it?'

His eyes glinted and a nerve flickered in his jaw at the implied insult, but he answered evenly enough. 'Nothing's wrong with Clover. It was on the market because its owners are getting on and have no family to leave it to.'

'So why did you buy it? Doesn't sound like your usual modus operandi,' she taunted.

He let her go and smiled, a cool chiselled movement of his lips. 'I bought Clover because you thought it was special, Kim. Goodnight.'

He retrieved his jacket, slung it over his shoulder and strode out.

CHAPTER FIVE

REITH RICHARDSON regarded his wife and took his time about it.

She was fairly tall, she was slim with a good figure and she was stunningly beautiful, with red-gold hair and sapphire-blue eyes. Her smooth skin was complemented by a pair of sparkling diamond earrings he had given her but was surprised to see her wearing. She usually made a point of refusing to wear any of the jewellery that came with the position of being his wife.

Of course, as a Theron of Saldanha and the Balthazar winery, the position of being his wife was a bit of a comedown for her, other than in monetary terms.

Her dress was cream and silky and long. It looked sleek when she stood still but when she moved it revealed yards of material in the skirt. With it she wore high nude platform shoes. But, beautiful as the dress was, as well as fashionable, it provoked one regret in him—it hid her legs and that was a pity; she had sensational legs.

In fact there was no doubt, so far as looks and an innate sort of classiness went, that she would be an asset to any man. In lots of ways she was to him but there was one downside—she hated him.

She blamed him for profiting from her family's misfortunes, she considered that she'd been manipulated into marrying him to stem some of the worst of those misfortunes. She despised his occupation, she'd accused him of having a questionable modus operandi—but in all other respects, bar one, she was a superb wife as, indeed, she'd promised to be.

She ran their homes perfectly, although she'd refused point-blank to live at Clover Hill. Out of necessity, he had moved in to Saldanha, though he was rarely there. She was an accomplished hostess so their social lives ran like clockwork and she was good with his motherless son.

And they all lived, like the old lady in the shoe, he thought with a wry twist of his lips, in Western Australia, south of Perth and towards the Margaret River district.

None of the Theron family, however, had approved of the Balthazar winery or the Saldanha estate straying out of the family, least of all his wife.

However, as he had once pointed out to her, she'd come with it and she *was* family. He'd also pointed out to her that, without his intervention, her parents—her father had recovered well from a heart bypass operation—would not now be settled in a fashionable unit overlooking the beach and bay, with its iconic dolphins, at Bunbury, enjoying a leisurely retirement. In fact they would have been much closer to a bedsit and Meals on Wheels. Nor would they have been able to afford the luxury cruise he had paid for, which had contributed significantly to Frank Theron's recovery from open-heart surgery.

She'd tossed her red-gold hair at him and her eyes had glinted sapphire fire but as he'd waited politely she'd clamped her mouth shut and stalked off.

Strangely, he'd taken himself to task for that encounter. How galling must it be to have things like that thrown into your face on a regular basis? he'd asked himself. Not that he did it often because, truth be told, he admired her fiery resolve not to forgive him for the proposition he'd put to her—marry me and I'll save your parents from bankruptcy.

Well, he amended to himself, he had admired that fiery resolve but he was starting to lose patience. Two months had passed since he'd married her.

'What are you thinking, Reith?'

Kim's voice broke into his thoughts. He grimaced as he saw the puzzled frown in her eyes, and shoved his hands into his pockets. 'That you look lovely; that you've been an accomplished wife and it's just a pity that you hate me. Let's see.' He pulled a hand out of his pocket, rubbed his jaw and looked out over the gardens of Saldanha in the slanting rays of the setting sun. 'What else was I thinking? I do appreciate how you've coped with Darcy; I do actually admire your hostility—well, I did—I'm starting to lose patience with it now.'

'What…what do you mean?' She frowned.

They were standing on the front doorstep. There was a gleaming gun-metal four-wheel drive parked on the driveway below them and they were about to go to a neighbouring property for dinner. Sunny Bob sat beside the car, ever hopeful that he'd get taken for a ride.

'This was never meant to be a marriage in name only, Kim,' he said, bringing his dark gaze back to rest on her.

Fresh colour stained her cheeks. 'I thought… I thought…' She stopped.

'You thought?'

'You promised me time,' she said more composedly. 'And I thought…you might change your mind anyway. You might find someone who suited you better. Or someone you actually loved,' she said with irony.

A dry smile twisted his lips. 'Is that what you were hoping? If so, you shouldn't have made yourself almost indispensable.'

Kim looked at him. 'Any good housekeeper could have done—'

'Not quite,' he broke in. 'They wouldn't care about Saldanha and Balthazar as you do or have taken the time with Darcy that you have,' he said dryly. 'You know,' he added, 'when we come home, we could take a walk through the garden in the moonlight—it's a full moon tonight—then I could take you upstairs and make love to you. After all, Kim,' he said deliberately, 'we *were* once on kissing terms.'

She took a ragged breath. 'I didn't know who you were.'

'That didn't affect the chemistry between us.' He looked down at her with something like contempt.

Kim closed her eyes because he was right and her objection had been unworthy—she had once kissed Reith Richardson with wonderful abandon, with passion and with promise—before she'd found out who he was. All the same…

She made a frustrated little sound and went to turn away.

He put out his hand and stopped her. 'And there was a lot more to it, as you damn well know.'

'Reith—' she looked pointedly at his hand on her arm '—this isn't the time or place to be having this kind of discussion.'

He didn't release her. 'You pick a suitable time and place then.' He shrugged and looked at her cynically. 'Provided it's within the foreseeable future and not a year down the track—or ten.'

She flinched inwardly at the insult. 'What I meant was…we're already running late for dinner.'

He did release her arm then and stepped back. 'You know, I never thought you were a coward, Kim.'

'I'm not,' she said icily.

'Or an ostrich,' he went on imperturbably.

'I'm not that either,' she flashed, her iciness turning to anger.

He shrugged. 'You could have fooled me. After you.' He stood aside.

She hesitated under the influence of an almighty desire to run away. But, really, she was like a puppet on a string and there was no way she could run away without breaking those strings. And the consequences of that could be catastrophic for her proud, dysfunctional family, whom she loved nonetheless…

She walked down the steps and got into the car.

* * *

It was a superb dinner.

Twenty people sat around the dining table. The meal had been served on exquisite porcelain and the wine had flowed out of crystal glasses. The tablecloth alone was a work of art, hand-embroidered with birds of paradise on ecru linen.

They were dining with their neighbours, Molly and Bill Lawson. Kim had known them all her life. She'd grown up with their children, all boys, and had been looked upon as a de facto daughter. That was still the case, which meant that Reith had been accepted without question, she thought darkly at times.

Then again, Reith could charm the socks off anyone when he set his mind to it and it wasn't only his dark good looks, his height and physique that did it. He had a way of making you laugh with a few wry words and a crooked grin. Sometimes he had a way of making you feel like the only person on the planet for him.

Not that her husband spent a lot of his life charming people, she thought as she put down her wine glass and pushed away her plate with nothing left of what had been a mouth-watering Bombe Alaska. No, impressing people was his other forte.

There was no doubt Bill Lawson, an astute judge of character with a good grasp of the business world, admired Reith greatly. There was no doubt Molly thought he was divine.

Why, oh, why, she sometimes thought, couldn't her parents have accepted Reith as the Lawsons had? Of course the answer was obvious—money and reputation and so much more had come into it, hadn't it?

She picked up her glass and took another sip of wine.

And now Reith had laid down a gauntlet.

Why hadn't she seen it coming? Because she'd been too immersed in restoring Saldanha to its former glory? Too busy doing the same for Balthazar?

Or *was* she a coward and had she been burying her head in the sand?

What if she…acquiesced? she wondered. Or—what if she confessed to Reith that she was never sure whether she loved him to distraction or hated him like poison?

There were certainly times when just to look at him or hear his voice brought on a deluge of anger as she recalled how beholden she was to him.

Equally certainly, though, there were times when she couldn't deny the potent physical effect he had on her. The times when—out of the blue, usually—she'd look at his hands and suffer the acute desire to have them running up and down her body. Times when she wanted to laugh with him and go into his arms to be held in affection and companionship and love.

Times when she longed to be in his bed, being made love to until she was sated and exhausted and slippery with sweat and…

She broke off those thoughts with a snap as something alerted her to the fact Reith was staring at her with a question mark in his eyes.

Oh, God, don't let me blush, she prayed, and was saved by Molly rising and gesturing towards the lounge, where the coffee tray was awaiting them. She rose swiftly and followed their hostess into the lounge.

* * *

It was midnight when the car turned into the long Saldanha driveway.

'Pleasant evening,' Reith murmured.

'Y…yes,' Kim agreed and could have shot herself for the slight quiver of nerves her voice betrayed.

He glanced at her and grimaced. 'You don't sound too sure.'

'I… What did you think of Chilli George?' she countered.

Reith pulled the car up opposite the back door and shrugged. 'Exotic—like her name, but then I suppose fashion designers need to be.' He paused, then he went on, 'Is that to be the extent of our conversation tonight, Kim? A dissection of Molly's guest list?'

Kim clasped her hands, then unclasped them as she struggled to find something to say, something that wasn't inane, that wasn't designed to ignore the situation between them, but no inspiration came. 'It's late,' she said. 'I… And…' She trailed off.

'Not the right time or place?' he suggested, his voice hardening.

She stayed silent.

'All right. Out you get,' he ordered.

'You could leave the car here, under the portico,' she said without thinking.

'I'm not taking it to the garage, I'm taking it to Perth.'

Kim jumped. 'At this time of night? Why?' She stared at him, wide-eyed.

Their gazes clashed. 'You're not really that naïve, are you?' he said with soft but patently lethal sarcasm.

'I…I… When will you be back?'

'No idea.' He drummed his fingers on the steering wheel.

'Reith!'

'Kimberley?' he replied politely, but with a world of contempt in his dark eyes.

She bit her lip, then got angry although she tried to rein it in. 'Suit yourself,' she told him coolly and got out but anger got the better of her and she slammed the car door.

It didn't help her state of mind to hear him laugh softly before he gunned the motor and drove off, sputtering gravel beneath his tyres.

The next morning, after what had felt like a sleepless night, Kim saddled her mare Matilda, affectionately known as Mattie, and went for a ride. Sunny Bob went with them and they headed for Balthazar and its Cellar Door, run on the estate and visited by wine-lovers from all over the world.

It was one thing she had always taken a special interest in, the Balthazar Cellar Door. Most wineries offered wine-tastings and sold their wines from their 'Cellar Doors' and many had restaurants as well as offering conducted tours through the winery itself. The Balthazar Cellar Door was housed in a stone and thatch building set in surroundings that were magical—gardens full of blooms, flowering creepers and trees, especially jacarandas, a stream that wound under wooden bridges, a thatched wishing well. And there was a natural amphitheatre backed by tall cypress-pines.

Inside, as well as the wine-tasting area, was the restaurant and a souvenir shop where she now worked several days a week, having given up her teaching job.

And as she cantered Mattie, then galloped her with their breath steaming in the early morning air as the pale colours of dawn smudged the horizon, it was Balthazar she was forcing herself to concentrate on.

Some wineries hosted art shows, some were famous for their music festivals. Balthazar held an annual fashion parade that was due in a couple of days. This year Kim had offered the opportunity to debut her spring collection to a new but dynamic Perth designer—the unfortunate Chilli George.

She grimaced as Mattie's hooves thudded over the turf. Not that Chilli was unfortunate in any context other than featuring unwittingly in the ongoing battle between Reith and Kimberley Richardson. She was in fact a petite, exquisitely chic blonde in her thirties. Perhaps she was a touch exotic but she certainly designed gorgeous clothes.

Kim owned some Chilli George clothes and they were fresh and exciting.

Was there something about Chilli that went beyond being a touch exotic, something she couldn't put her finger on that bothered her, though? she wondered, then shrugged.

Really, the designer was the least of her problems, she reminded herself, as she slowed Mattie to a walk as they did a quick tour of the Cellar Door and the winery itself as well as the gardens. Then she turned back towards Saldanha.

And as they got closer, as always, these days anyway,

it pulled at her heart-strings to see her home. Until a few months ago she'd taken Saldanha pretty much for granted. True, she'd always been appreciative of the lovely Cape Dutch architecture, brought from South Africa by a great-great-grandfather.

But although the sight of Saldanha pulled at her heart-strings, it was the carte blanche Reith had given her to renovate the estate that had saved her sanity in the early days of her loveless marriage. Not only that, it had brought to light skills she hadn't known she possessed, such as gardening. She was taken by surprise when the head gardener had approached her for instructions but, once the idea that she was in charge settled in, she took to it like the proverbial duck to water.

She supervised everything that went into the garden and everything that came out of it. She cherished her mother's and grandmother's beloved roses. She'd built a Japanese water garden with lilies and carp in the pond and stone benches under a jasmine creeper-covered lattice canopy. In the heat of mid-summer just the sound of water trickling down into the pond would be cooling.

Then she'd turned her attention to the house and looked around with new eyes. Saldanha homestead was still beautiful, it was still filled with furniture brought from South Africa in different woods—kiaat or teak, stinkwood, yellowwood—but it had got shabby and her parents hadn't been in the position to remedy that.

The first thing she did was have the house painted inside and out. She used some of her favourite colours, like chalk and lagoon-blue, mocha, raspberry, mango, mushroom and heritage green and some beautiful wallpapers, although she maintained white for the exterior. Then she'd pulled up all the fitted carpets and replaced them. Fortunately this was restricted to the second floor, as the ground floor and the main rooms had wooden parquet floors that were almost an artwork on their own. And she'd had all the bathrooms upgraded.

After this major upheaval, her efforts had been less disruptive—she and Mary Hiddens had had a great time modernizing the kitchen as well as replenishing the linen.

And after all the work and cherishing she'd lavished on it, on top of coming so close to losing it, Saldanha meant even more to her than ever.

But there were other things that weighed on her and filled her with a feeling of guilt at times—how lightly she'd taken everything that had made up her old life. Expensive schooling, then a gap year backpacking around Africa and Asia. University, all the right clothes, all the right friends, her horses, her parents' wealth.

She'd heard it said that Damien and Kimberley Theron went around as if they owned the district. She'd ignored the jibe at the time but now she was forced to look back and acknowledge that she may have, at times, behaved like a spoilt socialite.

If so, it sometimes helped to remind herself that at the grand old age of twenty-two she'd come to earth with an almighty bump. And she would never forgive herself for not noticing the dire straits her parents had got themselves into sooner.

Thinking of her parents led her to wondering—yet again—if Reith had sent them on a luxury cruise to relieve the pressure of their shock and disapproval about their daughter's marriage.

That's me, she reminded herself. And she had to confess it made things much easier because, since they'd got back, the sting and impossibility of it all seemed to have subsided.

Yes, her mother had several times tried to dig below the surface Kim presented of a busy, capable if not deliriously happy wife, until Kim had sat her down one day, taken Fiona's hands in hers and said, 'Mum, I'm fine. Please don't ask me to explain things between me and Reith…they're complicated but he's no monster and…I am fine.'

Fiona had grimaced, then said tremulously, 'I just wish we were a happy family again. I hardly see anything of Damien these days.'

'You're lucky to see him at all,' Kim had replied, then bitten her tongue. 'But you've got me,' she'd teased then.

And her mother had hugged her mightily.

One of the other aspects of her new life that was more rewarding than contemplating how things had changed for her, was dealing with Reith's motherless son.

For the most part, Darcy Richardson appeared to be a perfectly normal ten-year-old. Unlike his father, he was fair with hazel eyes and freckles, but it had struck Kim early on that he was just too perfect. He was polite, he had beautiful manners, he ate everything that was put in front of him and he came and went from his boarding school every second weekend with no sign of any regrets, no evidence of homesickness, no elation at being home either. In fact she got the feeling he was happier at school.

Once, Kim had involuntarily said to Reith as they'd dropped Darcy back at school, 'Is he a bit traumatized?'

Reith had stared at the image of his son diminishing in his rear-view mirror and, as she'd watched him, Kim had taken an unexpected breath.

There was not much she cared to admit she admired about Reith Richardson, but for one moment she'd seen a sort of suffering in his eyes she hadn't expected him to be capable of feeling.

'He...he can be a little hard to get through to sometimes,' he'd said.

'Because he lost his mother? And now his grandmother?'

Reith had accelerated the car down the school drive. 'He never knew his mother, but that's obviously a cross to bear for any child. Unfortunately, I haven't been able to spend as much time with him as I'd like to have.'

'That's not unusual for a father, a breadwinner,' Kimberley had said slowly. 'Perhaps especially without a wife. What about your parents? Did they help out?'

He'd cast her a look of such irony, she'd been jolted. 'My parents?' he'd said. 'My mother left home when I was ten and my father never recovered. He died before Darcy was born.'

'I'm sorry,' she'd murmured and one glance beneath her lashes at his harsh features had not encouraged her to pursue the subject.

It hadn't left her, though, and she might not have mentioned it or discussed it with Reith but from then on she'd taken a special interest in Darcy. From her interest in and experience with kids, she knew not to crowd the boy so she bided her time and watched what he did and how he reacted to life at Saldanha. It wasn't long before she noticed something that appeared to break through that excruciatingly polite, almost touch-me-not exterior Darcy Richardson presented to the world—a horse.

Mattie's half-brother, to be precise, a chestnut two-year-old Kim had often despaired of raising because of a throat deformity. But an operation had finally cured the problem and, although the colt was small and would only ever be a children's pony, he was now sound and just the right size for Darcy. What was more, she could see that Darcy was drawn to the chestnut.

'What's his name?' he'd asked Kim one day as he was scratching his forehead.

Kim grimaced. 'Rusty. Not very original but we didn't think he was going to survive.'

'Can he be ridden?'

'Sure—do you ride, Darcy?'

The boy had nodded. 'I get lessons at school. But they're all old hacks.'

'Would you like to ride Rusty?'

'Yes, if it's OK.'

'No problem, but we'll have to find a saddle and a hat for you. We'll go out together because he hasn't been ridden for a while and Mattie will be a good influence on him. And, just for safety's sake, we'll use a leading rein. But only until you've got to know him.'

So that was what they did, and got into the habit of doing it whenever Darcy was home.

Then one day Darcy had said to her, ‘Kim?’

She’d looked across at him in some surprise as they jogged through the paddock, because it was the first time he’d called her by name. ‘Yep?’

‘Can I give Rusty a new name?’

Kim blinked. ‘What did you have in mind?’

‘Rimfire!’

She’d scanned the two of them, the under-sized chestnut horse and his freckle-faced, enthusiastic rider and smiled to herself as she wondered what flights of fancy Darcy was indulging in with his horse. ‘Wow! Sounds super.’

‘Really? Do you really, really think so?’

‘Yes, I really, really do.’

The other thing she noticed was how Reith went out of his way to establish a rapport with his son, not entirely successfully, however.

Coming back to the present, the morning after Reith had driven to Perth in the middle of the night, she slid off Mattie and took some time to wash her down, dry her and mix her feed. Time, she understood, she was using to delay her return to the house, where it was much more difficult to ignore her problems…

‘Thanks, Mary,’ she said as the housekeeper delivered a laden trolley to the breakfast room.

Kim loved the breakfast room, with its view out over the herb garden. It had a stone fireplace, her mother’s desk, which she’d inherited, and some comfortable armchairs as well as the walnut dining table and chairs. The décor was beige walls, white woodwork and splashes of peppermint-green and rose-pink. Despite being labelled the breakfast room, they took all their meals there when they were alone.

Mary had been part of the Saldanha establishment for as long as Kim could remember and she was the soul of discretion. However, possibly because she'd known Kim since she was a baby, Mary also took a stance at times that advised Kim she liked to be kept up to date with 'movement on the station' and not only physical movement, a stance she demonstrated as she returned with the silver coffee pot.

'Mr Richardson didn't mention he was going away,' she said as she placed the pot carefully on a trivet.

'No,' Kim agreed. 'It…uh…came up out of the blue.'

'When will he be back?'

'I don't know,' Kim replied and grimaced at the sharp look she received. 'That is to say *he* didn't seem to know.'

Mary tidied the table unnecessarily. 'He didn't take any clothes.'

'Well, you know, Mary, we keep things in the apartment so we don't have to pack and so on.'

'The apartment in Perth? So that's where he's gone?'

'That's what he said,' Kimberley replied with a lilt, meant to convey complete unconcern, although, of course, Reith had said nothing of the kind.

But the housekeeper shrugged and went on her way looking reassured, although leaving Kim wondering whether she ever fooled Mary Hiddens.

She stared at her breakfast, bacon and eggs, then poured herself a glass of orange juice.

Fortunately, considering the state of her marriage, she mused, her parents had always had separate bedrooms.

Could they have any idea how handy that had been to their only daughter when she'd embarked on her marriage of convenience to Reith Richardson? she often wondered.

Mind you, she reminded herself, the other thing that helped conceal the true state of their marriage was the fact that Reith spent very little time at home. He'd had a helicopter pad installed behind the house and his royal-blue chopper was a common sight coming and going. He often left home ridiculously early or late, so it made sense for Kim to have her own bedroom. Well, she grimaced, more or less.

She thought about Reith's secretary, Alice Hawthorn, who was devoted to him. Alice was in her fifties, a widow, and secretly in love with Reith but a model of efficiency. She lived in Perth and worked in the office Reith maintained in the city.

If she had any doubts about her employer's marriage being made in heaven she never gave the slightest indication of it. But surely she must wonder, Kim sometimes thought. *She* has to brief me about all his movements, all the engagements we need to attend together—surely she must wonder if we ever pass the time of day with each other?

She shook her head and turned her attention to her breakfast, feeding most of her bacon to Sunny Bob, who grinned widely at her. Then she poured herself some coffee and found she was unable to tear her thoughts away from Reith and his dramatic departure last night, not to mention the gauntlet he'd laid down.

And with the memory of that came a cold little bubbling sense of fear brought on by the thought that if she didn't hold up her side of the bargain she would lose Saldanha and Balthazar. Not only that, but her parents could lose their pleasant lifestyle and her father could lose his position on the board of the winery, which seemed crucial to his self-respect.

Would he do that to her?

She sighed, a sound of pure frustration, because trying to read Reith was like trying to break a particularly difficult code.

Yes, the last few months had revealed that he was a tough businessman who invariably got his own way, but then she'd guessed that although she'd not known the full extent of it.

What had surprised her, as well as her father, who was nevertheless loath to admit it, was the depth and breadth of his vision in the cattle and wine business. It should have been new to him, she'd reasoned, the wine business anyway. But, new to him or not, what many saw as risks, he saw as challenges and some of his lightning decisions had taken her breath away.

She sometimes thought back to their first dinner, when she'd asked him what the appeal was in rescuing and buying ailing businesses. When she'd been, she thought with a private little grimace, a touch superior about vocations, and he'd answered that it was the challenge and the learning curve, or words to that effect. She now saw a powerful intellect at work as he absorbed knowledge like blotting paper.

She'd seen Balthazar pick up and only in seeing it did she realize she hadn't noticed its decline. She'd seen the Saldanha estate and the cattle it ran go through the same transformation.

She'd not known what to make of it when he'd complimented her on having a commercial instinct herself.

'What do you mean?' she'd asked rather sharply.

He'd grimaced and leant his wide shoulders against her bedroom door frame. She'd been sitting at her dressing table, brushing her hair as her final step towards getting ready for a luncheon they were hosting at home.

'It appears,' he'd said, 'that you could sell ice to Eskimos.'

Kim had been watching him in her mirror but she twisted on the stool and frowned at him. 'I don't understand. It sounds a bit fishy…'

He'd grinned. 'I shouldn't be surprised.'

'Why? What about?'

'That anything to do with commercialism has vulgar connotations for you.'

Kim had blinked several times. 'I said no such thing,' she objected.

'You didn't, but you didn't have to, you looked it. Or—' he'd shrugged and pushed his hands into the pockets of his trousers '—maybe it was just being compared to me in any way that you objected to.'

Kim had set her teeth as she rolled her brush in her

hands. 'Will you please tell me what you're talking about, Reith?'

'On the days you work in the Cellar Door shop, the takings increase by nearly thirty per cent.'

Kim's lips had parted.

'Which led me to believe you have a flair for parting people from their hard-earned dosh,' he added, 'to put it mildly.' He smiled.

She'd sucked in a breath. 'I don't do that. It sounds awful. All I do is—' she gestured '—make some suggestions.'

'Good ones, obviously. But if you have that kind of sales flair, you may have been wasted as a teacher, my dear.'

Kim had turned back on the stool. 'I enjoyed teaching,' she said, and lifted her brush, determined not to engage in any more infuriating conversation with her infuriating husband.

But her eyes had widened as he stepped up behind her and calmly removed the brush from her hand.

'Oh, much more genteel, teaching, I agree,' he'd said and threw the brush onto the bed, then ran his hands through her hair.

They'd stared at each other in the mirror, Kim wide-eyed and frozen. 'Looks much better a bit mussed up,' he drawled. 'Mmm—I could almost imagine that you've just got out of bed.'

He'd glanced significantly at her bed, she'd followed his glance and, to her horror, an image came to mind of the two of them writhing against each other, of her being wild and wanton in her love-making, electric but silken at the same time, and he wielding the strength of his beautiful body lightly at first and then more powerfully until…

She'd felt the breath rasp in her throat and a rush of sensation fizzed through her so that a pulse beat rapidly and she felt hot all over.

'Then again,' he'd drawled, 'I'd need a very vivid imagination, wouldn't I, Kim?'

He'd turned on his heel and walked out before she could think of a thing to say.

But when she'd calmed down, she had retaliated.

She'd appeared on the terrace where they were to eat, just as the first guests had arrived—with her hair tied back severely into a bun.

Only to see him looking stunned for a bare second, before his dark eyes had flooded with laughter.

She came back to the present and clicked her tongue because the whole incident still had the power to make her feel foolish.

There were other things that made her feel not so much foolish as—well, yes, she had to concede—like an ostrich intent on burying its head in the sand, but not in the way Reith had meant it. More to do with the questions she hadn't asked, about Darcy's mother, for example.

Where and how had he met her? How old had she been? He would have been about twenty-four. Had it been love at first sight? Was she the love of his life? Was that how he'd been able to propose a marriage of convenience to her? Because he knew he'd never be able to put another woman in Darcy's mother's place in his heart?

She finished her coffee and went upstairs to shower and change but her internal monologue refused to subside.

They were questions she *should* have asked, she told herself as she finished washing and turned the needle-sharp spray of the shower to cold so her skin tingled.

Yes—she stepped out of the shower and started to dry herself—instead of being as haughty about it all as only she could be, instead of being scared to the core of her being, but determined to put a brave but angry face on it, she should have asked some pertinent questions.

She rubbed her hair, then dropped the towel and reached for her underwear, matching bra and tiny panties in apple-green silk. She paused for a moment to consider her day—morning in the garden, afternoon at the Cellar Door, getting ready for the fashion parade—she donned jeans with a fresh pink cotton shirt and sat down at her dressing table.

These days, it often seemed like one of life's little ironies that she should, as a married woman, still be using the bedroom she'd used as a girl and one that was several doors away from the master bedroom. But in the early days of her marriage it had seemed like an excellent idea to stay put.

Anyway, in the early days, Reith had stayed at Clover Hill. And it was only when she'd explained to him, in casual tones but with her eyes an arctic blue, that if he thought he could bribe her into his bed by allowing her to believe he'd bought Clover Hill specially for her, he should have another think coming, that he'd retaliated by moving into Saldanha. This had caused her some frustration. Life had been easier the other way around.

But it was no longer a blue room, her bedroom.

Now she had ivory walls and white French colonial furniture on a thyme-green carpet. On one wall hung an intricate silk tapestry of a garden and a beautifully carved sandalwood chest stood at the end of the bed.

All of it couldn't have been further from her mind, however, as she rested her chin on her hands and voiced the thought she'd been fighting to avoid ever since she'd stepped out of the car the night before under the portico…

'Who's he with?'

Was it realistic to imagine that Reith was living like a monk while she held onto her pride? Or, as he himself had said, was that being naïve? But was there one mistress, or several?

What did she look like, if it was one? Did he prefer blondes or brunettes? Redheads weren't that easy to come by— Oh, stop it! she commanded herself. It's insane to be thinking these thoughts. It's crazy to be jealous of some faceless woman, or a dozen of them, for that matter, when for ninety-nine per cent of the time you hate the man.

CHAPTER SIX

THERE was no sign of Reith and the fashion parade was upon them.

Kim dressed in some of her Chilli George clothes, a gorgeous taupe silk tunic with long sleeves and a ruffled neckline and slim ivory trousers, but she kept her eye on the window as she dressed because it was apparent from the moment she'd woken that the sun wasn't shining for her…

It was raining, but not gently—it poured. It literally teemed so that just getting people into the Cellar Door from the flooded car park became an exercise in logistics.

Then there was a power failure and candles had to be lit before the backup generator kicked in.

'Keep the champagne flowing,' Kim's mother advised.

Kim grinned but agreed and it was a strategy that worked. The crowd remained good-humoured, despite all the delays and inconveniences.

Good humour was hard to come by behind the scenes, however.

There'd certainly been nothing in any of their meetings that had suggested to Kim that Chilli George would work herself into a state of near hysteria over the weather, the delay in getting the generator going and the non-appearance of her wardrobe co-ordinator and assistant, who'd both been caught on the wrong side of a flooded creek.

'Look, it doesn't really matter,' Kim said soothingly. 'The girls must know roughly what they have to wear.'

But suddenly she wasn't so sure as she looked around the colourful behind-the-scenes chaos of the dressing room. There were armfuls of clothes everywhere. There were cosmetics strewn across every flat surface. It was hot, despite the rain. There was a hairdresser torturing, by the look of it, one of the model's hair into ringlets with a hot hair iron.

'It matters,' Chilli stated through her teeth. 'The models need someone behind the scenes. You must do it, Kimberley!'

Kim opened her eyes. 'Do what?'

'Co-ordinate the clothes.'

'Don't be ridiculous. I don't know the ins and outs of the outfits, how they do up, what shoes— I've got no more idea of what goes with what than…than the man in the moon!'

'Then we must cancel.' Chilli flapped her arms, then buried her face in her hands.

'Don't be silly,' Kim remonstrated this time. 'I've got a hundred people sitting out there dying to see your clothes! They've paid a small fortune and some of them nearly *drowned* getting here. Look, I know you were going to compère and you probably know it off by heart, but if you've got some notes, I'll do that and you can stay behind the scenes and sort things out here.'

'Won't like that, but here,' one of the models murmured in an aside to Kim and put a sheaf of printed notes into her hand, a numbered description of all the outfits.

'No!' Chilli said dramatically. 'You couldn't possibly handle the compèring.'

''Specially not with the most gorgeous, sexy man I've seen for years sitting in the front row!' came another aside, beamed Kim's way.

Kim frowned and peered through a crack in the makeshift wall. There was only one man sitting in the front row to date—Reith, sitting with Molly Lawson, chatting away comfortably.

Kim stared at him through the crack and discovered she could have killed him. He was wearing jeans and a navy leather jacket. His hair looked damp but he was entirely at ease as he and Molly chatted. Not only at ease but, with his tall body squashed into a folding chair, he still managed to look formidably attractive, dark and exciting and enough to take your breath away…

Then they laughed, he and Molly, and she thought furiously—how dare you, Reith Richardson? How dare you carry on as if there's nothing amiss? How dare you not be here for *me* when I needed help with generators and all sorts of things earlier?

How dare you turn up now and steal the show so they're even talking about you backstage?

Then she froze because he looked up and seemed to

be looking straight at her. A tremor ran through her and she was rooted to the spot for a long moment until she turned away and made a decision—no hysterical fashion designer was going to dictate anything to her, let alone be offered the chance to drool over her husband.

She grimaced immediately as the irony of this hit her but it also hit her at the same time that that was what she'd been unable to put her finger on in Chilli George at Molly and Bill's dinner party—a very subtle but nonetheless perceptible interest in Reith. And she didn't care if it made no sane, rational sense but that annoyed her all the more.

She turned back. 'That's my last offer, Chilli,' she said coolly. 'But I'll help you pack up if you like, if that's what you really want to do. We'll have to refund—'

Chilli came to a hasty decision. 'No. But, for heaven's sake, get me a glass of…something and I don't mean a soft drink.'

Kim smiled more warmly at her. 'What a great idea! I'll have one too.'

Hours later, Kim drove back to Saldanha.

It had stopped raining but the night air was misty and cool.

She threw her car keys down onto the hall table, stretched, kicked her shoes off and hesitated.

She could see partly into the lounge, with its lovely lamps that Mary would have lit. With its beautiful rugs on the shining parquet floor, the linen settee covers and the bowl of magnificent roses on a drum table. And she smiled as she thought how well wine, grapes anyway, and roses went together.

But did she want to go straight upstairs to bed or did she want a nightcap to round off a difficult day? A nightcap to perhaps dull the sting of not knowing where Reith was. She'd seen him walk out of the Cellar Door after the parade and that was the last she'd seen of him.

She shrugged and wandered into the lounge, and stopped dead.

Reith looked up from the paper he was reading. There was a brandy in a balloon glass on the occasional table beside him.

He said nothing.

Kim came to life. 'That's where you are,' she murmured and walked over to the bar to pour herself a brandy.

'So we're talking? I wasn't sure,' he said dryly.

She merely looked at him and sat down in an armchair.

'OK, let's try this—you thought I should have stayed and helped? That's what you're mad about?' he queried.

She shrugged. 'It would have been a help, but no.'

'No? You don't think I should have stayed or—you're not mad?'

Kim tensed inwardly, bitterly regretting getting herself into this but she felt exhausted and didn't have the will to go away—where to, anyway? So she took refuge in her drink. She took a sip and stared into her glass.

'Next minute you'll be telling me there's nothing wrong,' he said softly. 'One of the all time favourite lies women employ when they're hiding huge grievances.'

She looked up, her eyes glittering like sapphires in the sudden pallor of her face. 'Of course you know this from your extensive experience of women, I presume?'

He laughed. 'Thought that might flush you out, my dear Kim. So, why don't you go on and spill the beans?'

'There's—' She closed her mouth, nearly biting her lip, and took another sip of her brandy.

'Nothing,' he said flatly. 'Is that why you didn't look at me? Not once while you were doing your stint on the microphone. Then or later. I might have been non-existent—'

'Why should I acknowledge you?' she broke in. 'I don't even know where you are half the time. I had no idea you'd be back for the parade. I had no idea where you went the two nights you were away but, no, I'm not so naïve as to imagine you're living like a monk.'

'I spent the first night, what was left of it, in the apartment, alone,' he said harshly. 'And the second night, last night, I got permission to take Darcy and some of his mates to a rugby game and they slept over.'

'That's—' her voice shook '—not what you intimated when you drove off.'

'No?' He stared at her with his mouth set. 'Then our lines must have crossed. I was intimating that spending another chaste night in this damn house with you was not going to work for me. That's *all*.'

Kim took several distressed breaths. 'I...I'm sorry if I got it wrong but—'

'Why would it bother you if I *was* sleeping around?' he cut in to ask with a frown. 'I thought you hated me.'

Kim stared at him. Then she got up and paced the

room. Finally she stopped in front of him with her arms crossed over her beautiful taupe silk top. 'Reith,' she said carefully, 'yes, there are times when I hate you quite…a lot.'

A nerve flickered in his jaw. 'I did save your family.'

'You could have done it differently.'

'No, Kim. I know what you're going to say. I could have given your father an active position—'

'Why not?' she broke in intensely.

'It wouldn't have worked,' he said flatly. 'You know as well as I do, he would have hated any innovation, he would hate anything I suggested. As for your brother,' he went on cynically, 'didn't any of you realize it's not wine and viticulture he lives and breathes, but horses?'

Kim flinched. 'Well…'

'Not only that—he's quite clueless when it comes to business.'

She walked back to her chair and took up her glass, turmoil clearly etched into her expression. 'I still can't—' She paused, then heaved a sigh. 'They're still my father and brother.'

Reith picked up his drink and looked sceptically into the tawny depths. Then he grimaced. 'It's hard to be objective about one's family, I guess. For example, I've gone the other way. I've never forgiven my parents, but—' he gestured '—be that as it may, what about the rest of the time?'

She blinked at him uncomprehendingly.

'You said there are times when you hate me quite a lot.' He looked sardonic. 'What about the other times?'

Kim hesitated, then sat down and finished her

brandy. She put the glass down precisely in the centre of the round occasional table. 'I…' She looked across at him and came to a sudden decision. 'Reith, I often feel I'm working without a script. You seem to know all my answers but I don't know yours. Tell me about your first wife.'

He raised an eyebrow. 'What do you want to know about her?' It wasn't said patiently.

Kim gestured. 'How you met. How long you knew each other, that kind of thing.'

'Kim, it's over ten years ago; it can't have any bearing on us.'

'Reith,' she said stubbornly, 'I want to know. I don't like being married to a stranger, which is what you are, to all intents and purposes. You always were.' Sudden tears blurred her vision. 'If you really want to know, I bitterly regret getting myself into this ridiculous position with you.'

'All right,' he said through his teeth, 'she was a country girl; she'd lived all her life on a cattle station. She would have been struck dumb in your company, but put her on a horse and she had her own kind of…class. Six months after we got married, though, we had nothing to talk about but she was pregnant and then…and then there was Darcy—but she was gone. She would have loved Darcy, but even more so because I think she knew—' He stopped.

'Knew you didn't love her any more?' Kim whispered, her eyes wide with horror.

He looked away. 'Yes, if ever. But she didn't even have that consolation.'

'And you don't think,' Kim said through her tears, 'that has left its mark on you?'

He stared at her with that nerve flickering in his jaw again. 'Of course. It has no bearing whatsoever on you, however.'

'You may not think so but,' she said tautly, 'I always knew there was an exclusion zone around you and now I know why.'

'That's nonsense,' he said roughly. 'I—'

'Believe me—' she interrupted '—if I'd had that kind of tragedy, or I'd caused that kind of tragedy in my love life, I'd have an exclusion zone.'

'Caused,' he repeated harshly and picked up his brandy glass and swirled it impatiently.

'Oh, not wittingly.' Kim gestured. 'Lots of people fall out of love or they were never really in love in the first place, or their love is one-sided. But it's enough to make you—' she paused as she gathered her thoughts, then, still pale but more composed, she eyed him as if struck by a new thought '—enough to make you force someone to marry you for all the wrong reasons, though?'

She let the question dangle in the air as she stood up, tall and elegant, with her red-gold hair a little dishevelled—just as he liked it—but her eyes very blue and steady.

'No,' she said, 'not enough for that. Not in my book. So what's left? The way my arrogant family treated you? Was that enough for you to force me to marry you? No. You can hold your own anywhere, Reith, even if it involves an old school tie and a polo team, and you know it.'

'So what's left?' Reith said as he stood up and faced her.

'What's left?' Kim murmured and shrugged. 'It's up to you. All I'm telling you is I don't accept that I should be obliged to make this a real marriage unless you can come up with a vastly better reason for it.'

She turned on her heel and walked away.

'Kim.'

She hesitated mid-stride, then turned back to him, a frown and a question mark in her eyes.

He was standing with his hands pushed into the pockets of his jeans. His deep blue shirt was open at the throat. He was tall and dark and enough to make you catch your breath even when you were questioning his every motive, his every rationale. Even when your heart was aching for the wife who'd died knowing he'd fallen out of love with her, if he'd ever been in love.

'Yes?'

'You didn't have to do it,' he said.

She licked her lips. 'You mean…?'

'You didn't have to marry me.' He waited to see her reaction, which was to suck in an unsteady breath. He smiled unamusedly. 'You could have ridden off into the sunset, so to speak, with your parents and your brother. At least your pride would have been intact even if you'd all been penniless.'

A tide of colour rushed up her throat and into her cheeks because, of course, he was right. But how to explain she couldn't have done it to her parents? 'I never wanted any of your money or *anything* from you,' she said hotly, 'but I couldn't do it to my parents; I just *couldn't*.'

He ignored the last bit. 'You haven't seemed to mind spending my money,' he said dryly, with a significant little look around.

Kim tossed her head. 'Don't waste your time trying to make me feel guilty about that,' she said proudly. 'You'd have got someone else to do it if it hadn't been me, but no one,' she assured him, 'would have restored Saldanha as well as I could.'

'Spoken like a true Theron,' he drawled. 'It's just a pity you don't—you haven't to date—made it a happy home.'

She shrugged. 'If you ever thought I was going to—'

'Lie down in a bed of your own making?' he interrupted sardonically. 'All right, let's talk about that, Kim.' He closed the gap between them in a few steps.

She stood her ground. 'Not *my* making,' she denied through her teeth.

'*Our* making, then.' He stopped in front of her.

She shivered but she knew immediately that she should have run, she should not have allowed herself to be trapped by the fatal physical fascination he'd held for her almost from the start. How *could* she still feel like this about him? she wondered in fleeting despair. Her pulse started to race as he stared down at her mouth and then his hands circled her waist.

'You said something about a "vastly better reason" for us to be married.' He looked into her eyes and his hands moved on her waist. 'There is, there always has been—and it's this.' He drew her into his arms.

'Reith—'

It was a breath of sound but he ignored it. She thought

he was going to kiss her, but he said, barely audibly, 'Remember doing this?'

Her eyes widened in surprise. 'I… Yes. I mean—yes, of course, well…' She closed her eyes and bit her lip in some confusion.

He laughed softly. 'So do I. It went something like this, didn't it?' And this time he did kiss her.

Kim tensed but he took his hands from her waist and cupped her face and trailed his fingers down the side of her neck—and all the things he'd made her feel came back to haunt her. Things she hadn't even been able to document to herself but now the memories of them, which must have lain just below the surface, were aroused. All her appreciation of his hard, honed bulk, the feeling of protection his arms around her had brought, the shivery delight caused by his fingers on her skin, the way her nipples flowered in almost unbearable expectation…

She was breathing raggedly as they drew apart and her legs felt unsteady. She was completely under his spell as she looked up into his eyes. There was not an ounce of fight left in her—she would have collapsed if he'd let her go, so great had been the impact of his kiss, so like a starving person brought to a feast had he made her feel.

Then, finally, a sound she knew well gained her attention. The familiar whirl of helicopter rotors as his company chopper settled onto the helipad outside.

'You… What… Where?' she stammered in disbelief. 'Is that for you?' She managed to sound more coherent.

He nodded. 'I'm off to Geraldton.'

'Did you know this?'

'Did I know I was leaving tonight? Yes. Kim—'

She pulled herself out of his arms. 'Don't let me detain you.'

'Kim—' a glint of amusement lit his eyes '—I'm sorry, I'd forgotten. You're not the only one somewhat… discomfited.'

'Oh, I'll be fine,' she assured him and shrugged. 'Just another of those ships in the night encounters we have from time to time.'

'Kim,' he said deliberately.

'No, Reith, I'm really tired anyway. Get Alice to let me know your movements if they affect mine. Goodnight.' She turned away as the helicopter pilot knocked on the back door.

But getting to sleep was another matter. She couldn't stop thinking about how she couldn't relinquish her opposition to the way Reith had married her but she couldn't stifle her attraction to him either… She couldn't quell her fears about the loner she sensed in him—and now knew it was not her imagination but a reality.

'I have to do something, though,' she whispered to herself as she dried her eyes and lay back. 'This is so… so unlike me.'

To make matters worse for her, when she did fall into a restless sleep it was to dream of Reith and a girl with Darcy's fair hair but with Reith always walking away from her…

* * *

She didn't come into contact with her husband for nearly a week and then more or less by accident.

It was five o'clock on a sunny afternoon and she was dressing to go to a neighbour's barbecue when she paused with her brush in her hand and a frown growing on her forehead. It wasn't the sound of the chopper she was hearing but in the clear afternoon air she could hear a vehicle coming up the driveway that sounded just like Reith's.

She walked over to the window and, sure enough, it was Reith—who was supposed to be in Adelaide.

She stood rooted to the spot, for some reason unable to move as she heard the car pull up, the front door open, then his footsteps on the stairs.

Thoughts raced through her mind: I don't know what to say to him—I haven't spoken to him since that evening!

'Kim? Are you home?'

She tried to say yes, but nothing came out. She cleared her throat. '…In here.'

He came in and her heart seemed to beat somewhere up in her throat just at the sight of him. She forced herself into speech to counteract that accelerated heartbeat.

'I thought you were in Adelaide.'

'I was supposed to be but—' he shrugged '—the meeting I had scheduled was cancelled.' He looked her up and down, her long ink-blue skirt, her chic hyacinth pink silk shirt, the wide turquoise belt emphasizing her narrow waist, her jewelled sandals. 'Going somewhere?' he asked with a lifted eyebrow.

Kim nodded. 'Pippa Longreach's barbecue. I did tell Alice about it but she told me you'd be in Adelaide.'

'I'd be in Adelaide,' he echoed. 'Just as well I'm not.'

'Oh?' she queried.

He smiled at her. 'I can keep you safe from Lachlan.'

Kim blinked. 'What do you mean?'

'You know very well what I mean, Kim. He may be Pippa's toy boy—' he grimaced '—but he's got a huge crush on you. Give me ten minutes; I need a shower.' And he disappeared into his bedroom.

Kim stared after him, prey to a host of conflicting emotions. She'd been dreading this encounter.

She was thoroughly conscious that on the night of the fashion parade what she'd set out to achieve—a fact-finding mission, in essence—had rebounded on her somewhat.

In other words, Reith's motivation for marrying her, other than physical attraction, was still unclear but her own motivation—her parents—had sounded, well, flimsy. Would it have been proudly foolhardy but somehow more—what was the right word—honourable?—to have turned his offer down?

She turned away, put her brush down and finished her make-up.

But of course—her hands stilled in the act of stroking mascara onto her lashes—her real fear about this meeting had been how she would react to him, how she would be able to defend herself against kissing him the way she had, if he called her to account over it, if he had that right.

She capped the mascara wand and picked up her

lipstick. But it had been quite normal, this first meeting after that night, she thought, as she painted her lips a soft luminous pink, then reached for a tissue to blot them. Would things stay that way between them, though, or was her moment of reckoning still to come?

CHAPTER SEVEN

PIPPA LONGREACH's barbecues were usually a lot of fun.

Pippa was an artist of quite some repute. In her fifties she'd divorced her second husband and was currently maintaining a toy boy who went by the name of Lachlan. He was ridiculously good-looking and well-built, with not a lot to say, however.

Although Pippa was primarily a painter, she was also a talented potter and screen-printer. Her home and its large terrace and garden showed off her art in many ways. There were pottery urns and statues in the garden and Pippa didn't only paint on canvas, she painted on walls, ceilings and doors.

She was also a gourmet chef and she grew a lot of her own vegetables, fruit and herbs.

Not only were her barbecues delicious, but they were also visual feasts and you never knew who you were likely to meet—from the famous to the notorious.

It was a starry night above the lively throng of guests and there were fairy lights strung through the trees, beneath which long wooden tables and benches had been set up and laid with colourful crockery.

A pig spit-roasted over a bed of glowing coals was part of the first course, accompanied by delicious home-grown roasted beetroot and corn, new potatoes in their jackets drizzled with melted butter and parsley, and a divine ratatouille. Homemade cob breads and real butter were on the tables.

As if all that wasn't enough, after a suitable interval Pippa served desserts, in typical Pippa style. She wheeled a whole trolley of them out: pavlovas topped with cream and passion fruit or cream and strawberries, a mocha soufflé, a brandy pudding, a sticky date pudding, orange glacé iced cupcakes…

Kim stared at the trolley, then turned to Reith, only to find him looking at her with comical disbelief, dismay and the same *will I be able to resist this?* expression that she wore.

She had to laugh and so did he.

He'd changed into jeans and boots and a cream linen shirt with patch pockets. During dinner he'd been good company but unobtrusively so.

Now, her smile faded and she turned away.

He drew a bottle of wine out of a pottery cooler and filled up her glass, then reached into an ice-filled tub, pulled out a beer and poured it into his glass.

'Cheers,' he said, touching his glass to hers.

'Cheers,' she repeated, still not looking at him.

'Hasn't been so bad, has it?' He narrowed his eyes as he watched for her reaction.

Kim blinked. 'No. I mean…I'm not sure what you mean. It's been a lovely evening.' She paused and frowned. 'Do you really believe what you said about Lachlan?'

Reith allowed his dark gaze to drift over to where Lachlan was sitting alone, looking magnificently moody, although he had been helping Pippa earlier.

'Yep.' He grimaced.

'But he hasn't been near me tonight and he's never said a thing to me that could be construed as…as anything but…OK.'

'Sensible guy,' Reith commented dryly.

'What's that supposed to mean?' Kim stared at him with a frown in her eyes. 'Surely not what I think?'

'Surely yes.' He shrugged and a fleeting smile twisted his lips. 'You don't honestly think I'd stand by and allow some overgrown hunk to pay attention to my wife? I—'

'Reith—' she broke in '—are you sure you're not imagining it?'

'Kim, no,' he said impatiently. 'I've seen the way he looks at you.'

She stared at him with her lips parted. 'Well, he's wasting his time,' she said at last. 'I don't like him, I don't like the way he's sponging off Pippa.'

'Pippa's old enough to be able to work things out for herself,' he drawled, 'but I'm glad you don't like him. Maybe, one day, he'll even be on the receiving end of some of your famed Theron arrogance— No—' he put his hand on her arm as she went to jump up '—don't. I'm sorry, I shouldn't have said that. Anyway, I wasn't talking about Lachlan or the party in the first place.'

She subsided and looked confused. 'What were you talking about?'

He paused and stretched out a hand to touch the gold bracelet she wore on her right wrist, giving her goose bumps as his long fingers played with the little links. And he seemed content to concentrate on what he was doing until, at last, he raised his dark gaze to hers.

'Us,' he said. 'Our last meeting was traumatic, to say the least, but it hasn't been so bad being in each other's company tonight, has it?'

A slow tide of colour mounted in Kim's cheeks and she lowered her lashes to hide the confusion in her eyes.

'You were worried about it?' he hazarded.

She could only nod after a moment.

'Of course, it's always easier in the midst of a crowd,' he suggested rather quizzically.

Kim glanced around at the 'crowd' but no one seemed to be taking the least interest in them. Then she looked directly at him at last. 'I…I suppose so,' she agreed.

'So, despite the fact that we make good sparring partners, we're also good in crowds, you and I.'

'What are you getting at now, Reith?' she enquired with a frown.

He shrugged. 'Just putting together a base table of the things we *can* do together.'

Kim stared at him and her lips twitched in spite of herself. 'You can't go very far on… That's only two.'

'I left out the most notable one. We'd need to be alone, as we were the other night until fate intervened—' he looked heavenwards a shade dryly '—to go into that.' He watched with interest as another tide of colour rose in her cheeks.

Kim bit her lip. 'I thought I might have to account for that—talking of base tables and things,' she added with a touch of tartness. 'I presume that's what you're on about?'

He played with her bracelet in silence for a few moments, then, 'Any thoughts you'd like to contribute? At all?'

Kim hesitated, then she said slowly and painfully, 'There is a physical attraction, but how do you know what the real thing is?'

'Love?'

'Yes.'

'You don't. Perhaps only time can tell.' He stared into her eyes.

'What was her name?' Kim heard herself asking barely audibly. 'Darcy's mother.'

She flinched as she saw the hardening of his expression and was quite prepared for him not to answer, but he said after a little pause, 'Sylvia. Sylvie or even Syl for short.'

'Did she... No.' Something inside her made her draw the line at asking him any more about Darcy's mother but it had also prompted her to think about his life at the time and before. 'You told me you didn't really grow up in a boundary rider's hut.'

He grimaced. 'No. But I did grow up on a remote cattle station. All the same, I went to the station school and my mother was a teacher so I had that influence before she took off for parts unknown. I'm told I was reading the Bible when I was four.'

Kim blinked as she absorbed this and at the same time absorbed the flicker of something cold in his eyes as he'd mentioned his mother. And she remembered what he'd said once about not forgiving his parents.

'So…so your father was a cattleman?'

He shook his head. 'My father was a chartered accountant who got caught up in a scam that was not of his making. He got barred all the same and never recovered from the shame of it all. He wasn't even a boundary rider, which at least sounds a bit romantic; he was the station bookkeeper.'

Kim stared at him with her lips parted. 'That's… awful.'

He shrugged. 'He certainly made heavy weather of it. He was cynical and untrusting.' He paused. 'If there was ever any joy in him it all got leached out. What persuaded my mother to stay with him as long as she did I don't know but the one thing I found hard to forgive her for was not taking me with her when she decamped.'

Kim's eyes were huge now. 'That's worse. So your mother ran away? How could she have left you, though? What was she like?' she asked with a frown.

'She was bright and bouncy, she was fun and she always tried to make the best of things. I think she came to know it was never going to work but my father would never let me go. She may even have thought he'd "go easier" on me if she wasn't there.' He shrugged. 'All he said when he read the note she left was, "Good riddance".'

'Did he go "easier" on you?'

'It wasn't in him to go easily on anyone.' He smiled dryly. 'It's all water under the bridge now, although—' he paused and narrowed his eyes '—you said something once about an exclusion zone. I think it was something Sylvie found she couldn't get through, while I couldn't even put a name to it or understand it; I think that in hindsight, at least. What a pity,' he said with considerable irony, 'hindsight couldn't be foresight.'

'Are you… Are you doing enough for Darcy, Reith?' Kim heard herself asking urgently after she'd thought all this through. 'I mean—why does he have to go to boarding school?'

Reith finally stopped fiddling with her bracelet and took a draught of his beer. 'It's a very good boarding school.'

'I'm not saying it isn't,' she replied impatiently.

'He seems happy there.'

'He seems too happy there,' Kim observed. 'I mean—' she gestured '—I get the feeling he's relieved to go back, although not so much now he's got Rusty—incidentally, I meant to ask you about that. The local gymkhana is coming up. Can I enter them? It'll be during the school holidays.'

'If they're good enough. What? Jumping? Dressage?'

'I'll look at the programme. He's really come along amazingly well—Darcy, I mean.'

Reith looked amused. 'He should. It's in his blood on both sides.'

'You ride? You rode—of course you did!' Kim

marvelled at her own stupidity. 'Why don't you ride at Saldanha?' She stared at him questioningly.

'Never seem to have the time.'

There was a whoosh as a bonfire was lit and flames and glowing points of light flew skywards.

Kim blinked and watched for a while but she had something on her mind, brought there by his story and the loneliness he must have experienced. 'Reith, why don't you bring Darcy home?' she asked at last.

Reith took a draught of his beer and put his glass down. 'Kim—' He stopped abruptly, then said deliberately, 'I can't guarantee Saldanha as a happy home for him.'

Kim clicked her tongue in annoyance. 'I have never shown the slightest animosity towards you in front of Darcy—and don't you dare dispute that,' she warned him with her most haughty expression.

'I wouldn't dream of it,' he said with mock meekness. 'But living together all the time is different.'

'Is that one of the reasons you married me?' she asked out of the blue as the thought struck her. 'If so, why didn't you say so?'

'You mean you'd have married me happily because of my son?' He tilted his head to one side to look at her quizzically. 'Pity I didn't think of that. Incidentally, Kimberley Theron—' he pressed on as she made to speak '—I had no intention of asking you to marry me.'

'Blackmailing me into marrying you, don't you mean?'

He rubbed his jaw. 'Whatever—until you took your family's side that day in the pub.'

'You expected me to…to take your side?' she said raggedly and gestured helplessly as she couldn't go on, so extreme was her frustration.

'I expected at least one of you to take a sane, rational, businesslike view of the matter,' he said coolly. 'I even thought we, you and I,' he said deliberately, 'had got on well enough for you to assess the facts first before you gave me my marching orders.'

Kim opened her mouth to say something bitter and pithy but she was reminded suddenly of her feeling of discomfort at the time when she was using her father's arguments—discomfort because they hadn't sounded sane, rational and businesslike?

'I also found it hard to believe you didn't know who I was,' he said.

Kim blinked several times. 'Come again?'

He shrugged. 'It was hard to imagine how they'd been able to keep it from you.'

She swallowed and drank some of her wine. 'That was partly my fault. I should have realized something was wrong.' She shook her head. 'I must have been blind. If it's any comfort to you, Reith Richardson—' her eyes were sombre '—there's an awful lot I've taken myself to task for since you—' she grimaced '—came into my life.'

'Change was going to happen for you anyway, Kim. It would have been someone else changing your life if it hadn't been me,' he said quietly.

A sparkle of amusement lit her eyes for one brief moment. 'They might not have wanted to marry me, though.'

She propped her chin on her hand and looked into the firelight for a long moment. Until it slowly dawned on her that Reith had gone very still as he stared at her. She had no idea that her profile was exquisite in the firelight against the darkened sky, that her skin was rose on gold, her hair more gold than red in the same firelight and her eyes like sapphires.

She lifted an eyebrow at him. 'Penny for them?'

He seemed to come back from a long way away. He finished his beer and said, as he put his glass down and squared it with the edge of the table, 'We don't need to be married any more, Kim. Oh—' he gestured as her eyes widened and she paled '—don't worry about your parents.'

'I don't understand!'

They were back at Saldanha.

They'd taken a distracted leave of Pippa—at least Kim had been distracted. Reith had been perfectly normal. And on the short drive home she'd struggled to find words through the utter sense of shock she was experiencing, whilst he'd said nothing at all and hadn't appeared to be struggling with anything.

'Reith,' she implored, all but tripping over her skirt and Sunny Bob as she climbed out of the car.

'It's over, Kim,' he said as he unlocked the door and gestured for her to precede him into the house. 'I'll move out tomorrow. That's all there is to it.'

Kim stalked inside and waited for him to do the same. Then she stopped him with a hand on his arm. 'Reith Richardson,' she said precisely, 'I've spent all the time I've known you on one kind of a roller coaster or another. Equally, I've had to make do with the limited information you see fit to feed me and I'm sick to *death* of it. So hand over my car keys. They're on the table behind you.' She put out a hand imperiously.

'Where the hell do you think you're going at this time of night?' he queried harshly.

'No idea! Maybe Perth—it seems a popular spot for midnight flits—but if you're not going to explain, I'm off!'

'Kim—all right,' he said through his teeth. 'There's no bloody point in going on, is there?' His eyes blazed. 'You're never going to forgive or forget. We could go on for years setting each other alight physically and spending every other damn moment fighting each other.'

She simply stared at him.

'Look,' he went on in the same hard voice, 'you're entirely in the right, if it's any consolation. I should never have done it.'

Kim opened and closed her mouth several times. And what finally came out surprised her. 'Wh...what about Darcy?'

If she'd surprised herself, she could see that she'd shocked him.

He blinked several times. 'I...' But he didn't seem able to finish.

'I haven't told you this, but I'm finally getting through to him,' she went on. 'He's even decided on a new name for his horse—Rimfire. What are you going to tell him?'

'I don't know—I haven't thought about it.'

She opened her hands. 'Ah. Another lack-of-information exercise in the making.'

He swore audibly. 'Better for it to happen now rather than later.'

'No,' Kim whispered with sudden tears in her eyes.

He studied the tears for a moment and a nerve flickered in his jaw. 'So what are you suggesting?' he asked with a frown. 'The same kind of hell we're going through, only a more amicable version of it for Darcy's sake? It's not going to work, Kim. We've wanted each other for months now. I don't know about you, but it's starting to drive me crazy. My only option now is to… go.'

'Why did you do it, Reith?' she asked, tears now streaking her mascara. 'Why *did* you ask me to marry you like that?'

'Because, despite what you might like to think,' he said curtly, 'I have a chip on my shoulder a mile wide, I probably always will have. And your brother and father were able to expose it in all its glory. Particularly your brother.'

She gasped. 'How? Why?'

'I could have understood your father's reaction to a certain extent, an older man with old-fashioned notions, but Damien…' He stopped and shook his head. 'They were so bloody superior when they discovered my background. Not only that, they made me feel like a scavenger when I knew damn well they'd dug their own hole and were responsible for their own downfall.'

'They were… It's possible they were just desperate, isn't it?'

He shook his head again and smiled with no amusement at all. 'Then you came along and you were all fabulous, rich, classy, sassy *Theron*,' he went on, and stopped, breathing harshly. 'Although one thing I have to salute you for, Kimberley. I thought you'd be much easier to seduce than you were. In fact, if there was a man with any backbone in your family, it was you.' And with his mouth in a hard line, he sketched a mocking little salute.

Kim's lips parted and for a moment something very much like stunned heartbreak showed in her eyes. Then she turned and started to walk away.

'Kim…' He said her name hoarsely but, with a slight shake of her head, she kept on walking.

'Kim.' He came round in front of her and barred her way and he put his hands on her arms. 'I'm sorry,' he said. 'I should never have said that.' He scanned her pale face and darkened eyes. 'I'm *sorry.* It's the way I am, though, it's the way I've been since I was ten.' And he pulled her into his arms. 'I'm sorry,' he said barely audibly into her hair.

She trembled and went to pull away but he resisted easily, then he picked her up and carried her through to the lounge and sat down on a settee with her.

He didn't say anything for a long time, just stroked her hair as she lay with her head turned into his shoulder.

And gradually the trembling that had attacked her eased and she lay against him feeling a strange kind of peace come over her. A release, almost, that puzzled her and puckered her brow briefly, then she realized what it was. Despite everything and after the long months of holding herself aloof, there was no other feeling for her that came close to the magic of being in Reith Richardson's arms.

As it struck her, her eyes flew open and she looked up to see him staring down at her.

'Reith?' It came out as a husky little breath of sound.

'Kim?'

They stared into each other's eyes for a long moment, then he pulled her close and started to kiss her.

The master bedroom at Saldanha was a beautiful room. It had a white ceiling, greyish-blue carpeting, mushroom walls and ivory curtains. The ivory silk bedspread hung over the antique ottoman and, by the light of the Chinese porcelain bedside lamps, Kim lay still as Reith paid tribute to the whole silken, slim, curved length of her.

But stillness wasn't going to stay with her much longer, she knew. Indeed, how she'd survived the way he'd undressed her item by item she didn't know.

Nor did she know how she'd contained her delight and awe at the sight of him powerfully naked next to her. The contrast between them was breathtaking. She felt slight and as light as air and vulnerable, but in a way that was thrilling to her senses, against him. He was so tall and tanned, broad-shouldered, lean and strong, his body sprinkled with dark hairs, his hands…

His hands, she thought with a visible tremor, so wise on her body, so sure in the way they found her most erogenous spots—she'd never be able to look at his hands again without remembering this—this sheer delight he was inflicting on her.

Then he eased his leg between hers and bent his dark head to taste and tease her nipples.

'Oh, Reith,' she whispered as she felt a deep clenching within her body. 'Oh, Reith, I'm dying. I need you.'

And he was there for her, with a mounting rhythm that she began to echo; one that carried them on a wave of rapture that exploded for both of them.

'So.'

Kim stirred and repeated his one word very quietly. 'So.'

He pulled a cover over them, took her in his arms and buried his head in the curve of her shoulder and they lay in silence, completely absorbed in each other and the memory of the event that had just taken place.

Then he asked a question. 'How the hell did we manage to abstain for so long?'

She freed a hand and ran her fingers through his hair. 'Basically, we're lookers not leapers.'

He laughed and kissed her. 'I feel as if I've leapt up a mountain.'

'I feel…' She paused and he lifted his head and rested it on his elbow so he could look into her eyes. 'You've made me feel more wonderful than I've ever felt in my life.'

'Kim.' He put his palm on her cheek and his eyes softened. 'I've no right to hear you say that. Not after—'

He stopped as she put her fingers to his lips. 'Let's not go back,' she whispered.

'I need to explain.' He kissed her palm.

But this time she replaced her fingers with her lips and she effectively silenced him.

Some weeks later, she got an early morning call from Alice. Reith had been away for a couple of nights, the first time they'd been apart since the momentous night of Pippa's barbecue...

'Kim, dear—' she and Alice had been on first name terms for some time now '—Reith would like you to be in Perth today and he said please dress up because he wants to take you to the races at Ascot. He's got a runner.'

Kim blinked. 'He didn't say anything about it to me.'

'No, he forgot. Funny that, he's been quite forgetful lately, quite...I don't know...as if he has other things on his mind.'

Kim's lips twitched as she thought of her powerful, usually completely businesslike husband having her on his mind to the point of being forgetful, and decided she liked that very much. But her smile changed to a frown.

'Alice, I've got to get ready—I've been in the garden. And it will take me at least an hour and a half to drive to Perth.'

'The chopper is coming to pick you up. Should be there in an hour, so that will give you time to get ready, then it's only a quick little trip and at this end a limo will pick you up and deliver you to Burswood.'

'Burswood?' Kim repeated, sounding surprised.

'The hotel. He's booked, rather I've booked a suite

for the night so you can pack a bag and leave it there. He'll meet you there.'

Kim frowned. 'Why not the apartment?'

'Have you forgotten, Kim?' Alice clicked her tongue as if she couldn't believe how forgetful they were both being at the moment. 'It's being redecorated.'

'Oh. Yes, I had,' Kim said ruefully. 'Well, I guess I'd better get cracking. Thank you, Alice.'

Kim arrived at the Burswood Casino complex on the banks of the Swan River with plenty of time to spare, and checked into the luxury hotel.

She unpacked her overnight bag, then checked herself in the mirror. She had on a black linen dress with short cap sleeves and a tulip-layered knee-length skirt. She had an oyster mohair jacket to go with the outfit as autumn slid towards winter and brought with it cooler weather. Her hair was loose but sleek and sculptured and she wore a string of pearls and tear-drop pearl earrings. Her make-up was perfect, and she lifted a fascinator out of the hat box she'd brought with her. It was a froth of dotted black veil on a comb and she slid it carefully onto her head.

She was studying her reflection, twisting this way and that with her hands on her hips, when the outer door of the suite opened and Reith came in.

He paused, saw her through the bedroom door and walked towards her.

She stayed exactly as she was as he stopped, paces from her, and their gazes clashed.

'Hello,' she said barely audibly.

His gaze roamed over her, from the top of her fascinator to the tips of her high black heels. 'Hello.' He pulled his jacket off and threw it over the back of a chair, then he loosened his tie.

'You didn't mention the races to me,' she murmured, conscious of a prickle of tension between them.

'No. I forgot. As I'm about to do again.'

She raised her eyebrows. 'What do you mean?'

He pulled his tie off and consigned it to lie on his jacket. 'The next time I decide to go to the races it will have to be in different circumstances.'

'I still don't understand.' Kim frowned.

Reith moved and put his hands on her waist.

She trembled as an inkling of his intentions came to her.

'It won't be after I've spent two nights away from you—put it like that,' he drawled.

'I see,' Kim said very seriously. 'In other words, you mean to tell me, Reith Richardson, that I've gone to all this trouble—' she sketched the outline of her figure, then touched her fascinator delicately '—for nothing?'

His arms closed round her waist, but he eyed her with some irony. 'Depends what you classify as "nothing". But I have also to tell you that even if I'd made love to you a couple of hours ago I would still be subject to an irresistible urge.'

'Urge? To?' she queried, wide-eyed.

'Undress you, disrupt you, dispense with all this exquisite grooming and finery, take you to bed.'

Kim stared up at him. 'You're serious.'

'Yep,' he agreed.

'Reith—' her lips twitched but her pulse was starting to race '—that sounds a bit…caveman.'

He raised her hand and kissed her knuckles. 'Not at all,' he said ruefully. 'Just some poor guy who can't seem to get enough of you.'

Kim laughed softly and kissed him, and she didn't object when he found the zip at the back of her dress and slid it down.

In fact she stepped out of it regally. And she dispensed with her black bra and suspender belt, her sheer stockings, then she remembered the fascinator with a little gurgle of laughter and took it off too.

He spanned her waist, then slid his hands up to cup her breasts, causing her nipples to peak like tight buds.

'Down to my pearls,' she quipped breathlessly, then promptly forgot about them as he looked down at her in a heavy-lidded way and with a nerve beating in his jaw that wreaked havoc with her senses.

She shivered with pleasure as he breathed harshly as if he was going to say something, but instead he made a growling little sound in his throat and swept her into his arms.

Everything became urgent from then on—urgent with desire. It was there in the way he got rid of his own clothes, in the way his hands and lips moved on her body. It was there in their breathing and their movements, the way she directed his hands, the way he directed hers. In the way they clung together as they climaxed, both helpless beneath the physical force of their union.

As they lay together, resting and relaxed, mentally

close as well as physically, it was perhaps half an hour before he said, 'Shall we do it?'

Her eyes widened. 'Again?'

'No—' he looked amused '—that might be a hard act to follow so soon. Shall we go back to Plan A?'

'You mean…' She sat up and blinked several times.

He nodded. 'Let's go to the races.'

They did just that, but while their undressing could not have been described as orderly, their dressing was much more leisurely.

Kim had the first shower in the en suite bathroom. He handed her a towel as she came out, kissed her on the lips in passing as he stepped in.

It was as he walked through to the bedroom, towelling his hair and with another towel slung around his hips, that he stopped and whistled.

Kim was wearing only a lacy black bra and a matching suspender belt and one sheer stocking. She was in the act of drawing the second stocking on and she completed the task but with a tinge of pink in her cheeks.

'Now that,' he murmured, 'is seriously sexy.'

She straightened. 'Think so?'

'Know so. It's also the first time I've seen you wear them. Do you wear them often?'

Kim shook her head. 'Not often, but some clothes just seem to cry out for you to be as elegant below as on the outer.'

'I see. Makes sense,' he murmured and raked his hand through his hair, then fingered his chin as if he was in two minds about something. 'Can I offer you some advice?'

She tilted her chin. 'If you like.'

He smiled slightly at the tinge of sheer Theron arrogance he saw in her expression. 'Put some clothes on—otherwise, despite what I said a few minutes ago, it could be back to Plan B.'

'Oh, dear.' Kim reached for her dress hastily and stepped into it. 'Is that better?' she asked innocently.

'No, it's not.' He took a step towards her.

'Hang on.' She tried to pull the zip up at the back but it jammed. 'Damn!' She looked over her shoulder as she tugged at it in vain.

'Here, let me help. You've got a bit of the lining caught in the teeth—there.' He pulled the zip up and slipped his arms around her waist from behind.

She leant back against him.

He said into her hair, 'OK. That was a close call but I think we could get this show on the road now.'

She turned around in his arms and laughed up at him, knowing that he caught his breath at the sheer animation of her expression, the wonderful colour of her eyes and hair, the lovely shape of her face, her smooth skin and tantalizing mouth.

Nor was she to know how close she had come to thawing the icy rock his emotions had become, how close to lightening the darkness that had invaded him a long time ago and grown within him.

But would he ever come to completely trust her? he wondered. And frowned suddenly. What did he mean by that? Was he always going to wonder if she would revert to her roots? In other words, decide or be persuaded he was not good enough for her? Would he ever entirely forget the encounter that had prompted him to force her to marry him?

'Reith?'

He came out of his reverie to see her looking questioningly up at him now. Questioningly and soberly.

'Nothing.' He kissed her and released her.

CHAPTER EIGHT

THEY had a fun afternoon at the races in the Members' Enclosure. Reith's horse came second and Kim picked two winners. They drank champagne. The fashions, the glossy horses and the colourful jockey silks contributed to a gala feeling. Then there was the green sweep of the track with the glint of the Swan River in the background, the children playing on the grass, the blue sky above—all of it gave Kim a feeling of being on top of the world.

But the other reason for her feeling of well-being was their closeness. They rarely left each other's side and, once, she turned to him to find him looking down at her intently and in a way that made her colour slightly.

He smiled and slid her hand into his and, although they didn't say a word, their mental unity was complete.

The only thing that might have spoilt the day for Kim was catching sight of her brother, Damien.

He was with a gorgeous, very expensive-looking blonde in a party of six and if he saw her he gave no sign of it. She half lifted her hand to wave to him as he looked her way once but he looked away immediately.

She turned away with an inward shiver.

Whereas their father appeared to be reconciled to the idea of her marriage to Reith, Damien still hadn't forgiven her, much to their mother's ongoing distress. Kim couldn't understand why. Had he also hoped for some kind of a miracle to save them? Or was it the blow that had been administered to his pride by having his sister marry the man who'd exposed his lack of business acumen?

He'd moved his polo ponies out of the Saldanha stables and never came back to visit. He had, according to their mother, bought into a bloodstock agency.

It also struck her that Damien could rightly have expected to inherit Saldanha and seeing her in his place could be a thorn in his side. There was nothing she could do about it, though, and she deliberately pushed it from her mind.

In this she was aided by the fact that they picked Darcy up from school on their way home to Saldanha. It was a half-term holiday, and she was able to implement a plan she'd had in the making for some time.

Her first action some weeks ago had been to advise Alice that she needed Reith home for the three days of Darcy's half-term holiday. She had asked his secretary to make sure that Reith was appointment- and travel-free. Alice had been only too happy to comply.

Her next line of action had been to select a horse suitable for Reith and have it brought in from the paddock. She'd then groomed it and ridden it herself a couple of times.

The end result was that on the morning of the day

after they'd picked up Darcy, they loaded their horses onto a truck and took them down to the beach for a gallop.

It was a cool overcast day with showers etched like pencil lines over the ocean as it pounded against the shore.

They cantered side by side, rising rhythmically in the saddle on the hard sand left by the outgoing tide, with the balls of their feet planted firmly in the stirrups.

She and Darcy were bundled up in anoraks and tracksuits, while Reith wore a navy jumper and jeans. He looked completely at home on his horse, although he'd been a little taken aback on discovering what her plan was.

'I haven't ridden for years,' he'd said.

'It's not something you forget,' she'd replied.

He'd looked across the breakfast table at her with a faint frown. 'Something I wanted to ask you. You wouldn't by any chance be behind the fact that I have absolutely no appointments at the moment?'

'I?' She'd looked at him, wide-eyed.

'Yes, you.'

She was saved from answering by Darcy, who could barely contain his excitement at the prospect of a gallop along the beach. 'I'm sure Rimfire will love it. Has he ever seen the sea, Kim?'

'No,' she said, 'don't think so. So he may be a bit puzzled at first. Just take it slowly.'

'I will. I can't wait!' And he'd turned a glowing face on his father. 'Would you like Kim to take you on a leading rein for a while? She did that for me, just for the first couple of times until I was sure of myself. She's a really, really good rider,' he assured his father.

Kim had struggled not to laugh at the fleeting expression that crossed Reith's face before he brought it under control.

'I think I'll be OK,' he said gravely to his son.

Darcy shrugged. 'You did say you hadn't ridden for years.'

'True,' Reith agreed, 'but I still think I'll be OK.'

Back on the beach, Kim dropped behind after they'd had an exhilarating gallop through some light showers and she walked Mattie, patting her horse's steaming neck, while she watched Reith and Darcy splashing through the shallows.

Would this bring them together? she wondered. Would this common interest, assuming she could pin Reith down long enough to make it a common interest, be the bridge he needed to get through to his son?

Later that day, after Darcy had gone to bed and when they were getting ready for bed themselves, Reith, if not so much answering her question, acknowledged the thought behind it.

'You're clever, you know.'

She was sitting before her dressing table smoothing moisturizer into her skin. Her long nightgown was the finest pearl cotton, pintucked across the bodice and with frills at her wrists. It was also the height of modesty.

She turned on the stool and studied him. He was lying back in bed with his pillows pulled up behind him.

His pyjama jacket was unbuttoned, exposing his lean torso sprinkled with dark hair. He looked, in a word, she thought with an inward tremor, sexy.

'Clever? How so?'

'I never thought of horses as a means of getting through to Darcy. I've tried surfing, rugby, golf, athletics—' He broke off and grimaced.

She lifted her shoulders. 'That's probably only because you hadn't seen him exposed to them before.'

'Mmm…' He didn't sound convinced. 'I'm thinking of bringing him here now.'

'Oh, Reith!' She glinted him a radiant look. 'I'd love that and I think maybe he would too.'

He was silent for a long moment. 'Come to bed,' he suggested at last.

She did as requested, turning off the lights, except the bedside lamps.

'This is a very…old-fashioned item of nightwear,' he commented as she pulled the covers over her.

'Ah, but it cost a small fortune,' she replied. 'It's handmade, it's light but warm now the nights are getting chilly and it's comfortable. My mother has a lady who makes them and it's a pattern that came down from my great-great-grandmother.'

'So the history goes back even to what you wear to bed?' He paused, then said, 'If there's one thing I've come to understand through all this—' he took his fingers from her hair and fingered the material of her nightgown '—it's… I guess your nightgown encapsulates it.'

She frowned. 'What do you mean?'

'When there's as much history involved as there is here, there has to be a terrible, tearing sense of loss at the thought of losing it, however it happens.'

Again it was ages before Kim spoke and then it was with tears in her eyes. 'Thank you for that,' she said huskily, and she reached for his hand and kissed it.

'Of course,' he said, 'you do realize, history or none, that I'm going to take it off?'

She smiled and released his hand. 'My nightgown?'

He cupped the curve of her cheek. 'Uh-huh. I'm still a guy who can't get enough of you, I'm afraid.'

'Mr Richardson,' she replied seriously, 'which is how I would have addressed you in my great-great-grandmother's time, incidentally, be my guest.'

It was in the languorous aftermath of their love-making that he made another suggestion. 'Since you have me at your mercy for the next two days, will you come to Clover Hill?'

Kim stiffened slightly.

'Only to have a look around,' he said. 'I was thinking of taking Darcy. After all, it'll be his one day.'

Kim moved her head on his shoulder. 'All right,' she said slowly. 'Is anyone living there?'

'No. But it's being looked after.'

'All right,' she repeated, and relaxed as his arms went around her. What could it hurt? she thought, and fell asleep feeling loved and cherished.

* * *

That's what they did the next morning.

Sunny Bob went with them, and Darcy, in his new role of horse-lover, was visibly impressed.

Impressed by the three powerful stallions standing at Clover, by the mares and foals, the paddocks, the stables, all of which made the Saldanha horse presence look small.

Not only that, but he seemed to have a way, particularly with the foals, prompting Reith to say to him, 'You take after your mother.'

'Do I? How?'

'She was especially good with young horses. She…'

Kim found she had sudden tears in her eyes as she watched the two of them standing side by side and, as Reith went on to speak to Darcy about his mother, she melted away and took herself up to the house.

It was a two-storey creeper-clad house set on a slight rise which gave it a marvellous view, not only of the paddocks and surrounding countryside but the hills as well.

As Kim walked through the silent rooms, still partly furnished, not only the view impressed her but a strange feeling of peace came to her.

The reason it was partly furnished was because the previous owners had not been able to fit all their furniture into their new smaller home, but the lovely old pieces they'd left behind looked to be part of the house, part of its history. And although it didn't have the uniqueness of Saldanha with its distinctive Cape Dutch architecture, it was, as she'd sensed all those months ago, as special as the rest of the property.

She wandered upstairs and was charmed to find a nursery with a beautiful cherrywood cot and Mary Poppins flying round the walls.

There was a sewing room with a marvellous old treadle sewing machine, a linen press the size of a small room, an empty master bedroom that opened onto the veranda and just beyond it a huge jacaranda tree that would be a sight to behold in spring.

Downstairs, all the main rooms—library, lounge, dining room—opened onto the veranda, only a step above the formal gardens.

Kim strolled out into the garden and looked around. She was proud of her garden at Saldanha but even it couldn't rival the sweeps of lawn between beautiful old trees and the riot of colour in the vast beds of winter-flowering bulbs: daffodils, jonquils, hyacinth, narcissus, tulips, irises.

Nor could it rival the secret paths that led to separate areas with different plants: native plants, perennial beds, succulents, grevilleas.

And then there were the roses.

She was simply standing, drinking in the rose garden with the house behind it and wondering at the same time why the peace and tranquillity of Clover was so… so mesmerizing.

Did it have a more peaceful history than Saldanha?

That wouldn't be hard, not lately, anyway, she thought with a frown.

'There you are.' Reith and Darcy with Sunny Bob

came into view. 'What do you think of it?' Reith went on to ask.

'It's—' she paused and wondered how to do Clover justice '—beautiful.'

Reith looked at her intently for a long moment, but said nothing more on the subject and they strolled back to the car.

But Darcy was in good form. He didn't stop chatting all the way home about everything he'd seen, about how his dad thought he took after his mum, and Kim couldn't help marvelling at the difference in him. He'd changed from the quiet, self-contained child she'd first met to this eager, bubbling ten-year-old.

If nothing else good had come out of all the Saldanha strife, she caught herself thinking, Darcy had benefited so much.

Over dinner that night Reith enquired of her what she had planned for the next day.

Kim had cooked dinner—it was Mary's day off—and she'd served it in the breakfast room: steak, eggs, chips and a salad.

'Boy, oh, boy!' Darcy commented soulfully as he looked at his plate, 'you really, really know how to feed a kid, Kim.'

'Really? Thank you,' she replied, looking gratified.

That was when, with an amused grin, Reith asked his question.

'Nothing,' she replied. 'Well—'

'Thought you must have something planned,' Reith interrupted.

'I don't, but—'

'Highly unlikely for you not to have,' he broke in again.

Kim planted her fists on the table, with her knife and fork most inelegantly upright in them. 'Will you let me finish?'

'Yes, Dad,' Darcy said severely, 'it's rude to keep interrupting.'

'I stand corrected!' Reith looked rueful. 'You have the floor, Miss Theron.'

'I…'

But this time it was Darcy who interrupted. 'Why do you call her that?'

'He calls me that to annoy me, Darcy,' Kim said, shooting Reith a dark glance, 'but if you'll both desist, I thought that between you, you two, you could decide what you want to do tomorrow.'

'Ah,' Reith said.

'Wow!' Darcy said.

'So what'll it be?' She glanced from one to the other.

'How about,' Reith said thoughtfully, 'we take the chopper out to Rottnest?'

Rottnest Island, just eighteen kilometres off Perth in the Indian Ocean, with its secluded beaches and bays and its great surfing spots, was a tourist destination accessible by big ferries as well as helicopters and light planes. Darcy loved every minute of their time there.

Rotto, as it was affectionately known to the locals, was a car-free zone so they hired bicycles and explored some of the beaches, stopping to swim in the turquoise waters, as well as looking at some of its history, early buildings and the lighthouse.

They bought lunch from the famous local bakery and went quokka hunting, looking for the furry little marsupials for which the island was also famous.

Then, tired but exhilarated, they flew directly to Perth, where they dropped Darcy off at his boarding school and, for the first time, Kim detected a reluctance in Reith's son to go back.

He even hugged them both and extracted a promise from Kim to look after Rimfire, as well as thanking Reith for a really, really super day.

As the helicopter lifted off, Kim said to Reith, 'When will you bring him home?'

'At the end of the term. We'll have to decide what school to send him to in the district.'

She nodded. 'There are several.' And she found herself thinking out of the blue not so much of Darcy but, no doubt prompted by him, about being a mother herself, about starting a family. Probably a good idea not to leave it too long, from Darcy's point of view if nothing else.

She glanced at Reith. He was piloting the chopper himself on this occasion and concentrating on his flying.

'How do you feel about more children?' She put the question into words.

He glanced at her. 'I don't think we need to rush into it. What do you think?'

'Hmm,' she temporised, 'perhaps not.'

'We've only just got Darcy more or less sorted,' he added. 'We haven't even got him home yet.'

Kim stared straight ahead and wondered if she was imagining it, an undertone in his voice, a rather stark undertone that meant—what? That he wasn't that keen on having more children ever?

Then he was talking to an air-traffic controller through his mike and she was left thinking it was strange that they'd never discussed it before. Come to that there was quite a lot they'd never discussed. In fact, she mused, you could say their relationship was more like an affair from that point of view, couldn't you?

But she said no more and they flew home. And, despite the things they hadn't discussed, Kim found herself concentrating on the high points of the half-term weekend and feeling contented, with little inkling that it was to be short-lived.

The next morning Reith had an early appointment and would be away overnight. She gave him a quick kiss and told him to be back soon.

'No, you don't,' he told her. 'I need to be properly farewelled.'

She looked up at him, her blue eyes alight with laughter. 'You sound like some potentate.'

'Not at all,' he denied and put his arms around her.

'You're certainly well-dressed enough to be one.' She stood back a bit and studied his beautifully tailored navy blue suit with a navy waistcoat over a pale blue shirt and a lavender paisley tie and matching handkerchief in his breast pocket. Then she looked at him with a question mark in her eyes.

'A board meeting,' he supplied. 'Then lunch.'

'No women at either, I hope!'

He frowned. 'Probably. Why?'

'I don't think I should let you loose. They'll probably keel over in the aisles for you.'

'Kim—' he looked at her askance, as if not sure whether to take her seriously '—that's highly unlikely.'

'Oh, I don't know,' she said airily. 'I had it once on good—make that *very* good—authority that you were the most gorgeous, sexy man in the room—or words to that effect.'

He blinked. 'When?'

'The fashion parade.' She described the scene for him.

He started to laugh. 'Well, that explains it,' he said, still grinning.

'Explains what?' Kim raised her eyebrows.

'You were exceedingly angry with me that day. Remember?'

'Mmm…' She looked somewhat rueful. 'You're right. At the time, the fact that some exceedingly glamorous female thought you were God's gift to women did not appeal to me in the slightest.'

'You don't think it was a bit unfair to blame me?' he queried, his eyes wryly amused.

Her lips twitched. 'Not at all. OK—' she leant against him, put her hands on his shoulders and kissed him lingeringly '—off you go.'

He went but not before returning her kiss with extreme thoroughness so that she was both thrilled and shaken in roughly equal proportions, and quite distracted for the rest of the morning.

But part of her distraction, she felt, came from some curious mood swings. One moment she felt on top of the world, the next she could be deeply emotional. Only the day before, she'd discovered a dead bird in the garden, a colourful parrot that must have flown into a high wire and broken its neck. She'd wept as she'd buried it and been sad for hours.

Was it all to do with being deeply—and she couldn't doubt she was—in love? Was that why colours seemed brighter and small tragedies seemed darker?

Her mother came to morning tea that day.

Kim had never fully explained her marriage to Fiona. All the same, she'd assumed that her family understood there had been some sort of quid pro quo involved, although she'd subsequently refused to discuss it with any of them. How could you explain to your family that you'd been blackmailed into marriage on their behalf?

But now she could see that her mother was less troubled by it; in fact lately Kim had got the impression that she would like to give them her blessing.

It wasn't Reith that their discussion turned to, though, over Mary's special carrot cake and herb tea—it was Damien.

CHAPTER NINE

'I SEE so little of him,' Fiona said sadly.

Kim stirred her tea. 'He ignored me at the races. He was with a very exotic-looking blonde. Is he serious about her?'

Fiona shrugged. 'I don't know. He hasn't said and needless to say, I haven't met her.'

'At least bloodstock should suit him,' Kim murmured after a thoughtful pause between them, and was horrified to see her mother wiping away a tear. 'You're really upset about Damien—I wish there was something I could do.'

'In the end, all you really have is your family,' Fiona wept. 'I've learnt that lesson the hard way.'

Kim took herself for a ride after her mother had gone. It was a cool day, cloudy but with occasional patches of sunlight. The Darling foothills lay like sleeping behemoths on the western horizon beyond the dun winter paddocks.

As Mattie cantered towards a shallow creek, then splashed across, it seemed as if the birdsong, the thud of Mattie's hooves, the reins between her fingers and the creak of her saddle were the limits of her world.

She pulled up and dismounted alongside a huge gum tree with a water trough for stock beside it and a hitching post. There were also several tree stumps that made good seats.

She sat down on a stump after she'd let Mattie have a drink and tied her loosely to the hitching post. She stripped off her gloves and got up again to pull a slim plastic bottle of water in a padded container out of her saddle pocket. It had been iced water, it was now chilled water. She sipped as she sat back down on the tree stump and thought—*think, Kim!*

There's got to be something I can do to get Damien back. But how? And what would Reith think?

It struck her again that she still found Reith hard to read at times. Since the night they'd first made love there'd been no explanations—well, she herself had stopped him from explaining anything that night. But since then they'd said nothing about how they felt about each other, other than in a physical context. They hadn't discussed their life, they hadn't made any plans excepting his plans for Darcy, although now she did have the distinct impression he wasn't that keen on having more children.

But when he wasn't home, she went about her life much as she had ever since their marriage.

She spent the usual amount of time at Balthazar, in her garden, she entertained.

She had not, she realized suddenly as she watched Mattie switching her tail to discourage the flies, other than her quiet joy in their closeness, considered whether she would love Reith Richardson for ever, whether he loved her madly, as opposed to desiring her madly.

She'd lived from day to day, in other words, almost as if in a bubble, a bubble she shouldn't test or probe too much in case it burst on her…

But surely mending some fences with her brother couldn't burst the bubble? No, she wouldn't allow it to. She wouldn't allow Reith to dictate a stance to her on the subject of her brother. She would explain her mother's hurt, her own hurt, come to that. They may not have been that close but he was still her brother, he'd taught her to ride and, come to think of it, he'd vetted her boyfriends once she'd got to high school. Maybe it was a habit he hadn't got out of, she thought with a grimace.

In any event it saddened her, suddenly and tremendously, she realized, to think of Damien cut off from his family. And she was going to have to do something about it.

Later that day, dressed in a dark, warm but stylish trouser suit and with a small overnight bag, she got out her car. To his delight, Sunny Bob was invited to accompany her, and they set off for Perth.

The apartment was still being renovated, but that suited her. She didn't feel like encountering Reith until she'd laid her plans.

She booked into a handy motel, one that took dogs, then drove into the city centre, where Damien had an apartment.

She parked her car as close as she could get to the

building, which was not that close, but she decided a walk would help her crystallize her thoughts and decide what she was going to say to her brother.

A couple of hours later, she strolled back towards her car, marvelling at the revelations that had come from her meeting with Damien.

At first he'd been prickly and defensive and obviously not that happy to see her. Then, when she'd refused to take offence, he'd poured them both a drink and with a sudden harsh sigh, had told her that for most of his life he'd been trying to live up to their father's expectations of him as a wine-maker, when his heart wasn't in it. And then along had come Reith Richardson, who'd exposed not only his deficiencies as a wine-maker and a businessman but had married *her*.

'He made me feel so stupid,' he'd confessed.

'Deliberately?' Kim had enquired with a frown.

'No, not really,' Damien had conceded, 'but I could see the sheer acumen and the drive in him that I wouldn't ever have. Not unless it had to do with horses. And, on top of being about to lose Balthazar and Saldanha to him—well, I'm sorry, Kim—' he'd looked directly at her '—but there seemed to be only one way I could go and that was to hate him and try to belittle him through his background—or lack of it.'

She stopped walking and shook her head, still absolutely amazed at the complexities life threw up. She'd never imagined her suave, worldly brother—or that was how she'd seen him—could feel so inadequate. But at least she was several steps closer to reuniting the family. If only she could explain it all to Reith now…

She started to walk again and what she least expected to see was Reith coming out of a luxury hotel lobby with a woman beside him.

Not any woman, she saw, as she edged into the shadows along the inside of the pavement, but Chilli George.

A taxi was waiting at the kerb and Reith opened the door and gestured for Chilli to get in but she didn't, not immediately. She picked up Reith's free hand and placed it over her breast, and for a long moment both of them seemed to be etched in stone as they stared into each other's eyes. Then Reith took his hand away and Chilli got into the limo. Reith waited for it to draw away from the kerb before he turned and went back into the hotel.

Why didn't she just confront Reith? Kim wondered.

She'd gathered herself together after the little scene outside the hotel and she was back in her motel.

She'd brewed herself a cup of coffee but she wasn't sure why. Drinking coffee was the last thing she felt like doing. In fact the thought was thoroughly nauseating but what she really wanted to do—scream, shout, throw things, even smash things—was not permissible.

How *could* he?

When their marriage appeared to be going so well, when Darcy was coming to live with them, how could he be with another woman, but especially Chilli, she thought furiously, who had a reputation for chasing men?

And from fury she went to sorrow and found tears rolling down her cheeks.

Darcy—how would Darcy react? Would he go back

into his shell if she and Reith broke up? she wondered as she tried to stem her tears with a tissue.

Would it come to that?

But how could she go on with him if she could never trust him again?

She got up suddenly with a hand to her mouth, then rushed to the bathroom where she was sick.

Emotion, she thought, as she rinsed her mouth and studied her pale, mascara-streaked face in the mirror.

Or…?

She whirled on her heel and ran to find her purse. She dragged her diary out of it and, with trembling fingers established, to her disbelief, that her period, which usually came and went like clockwork, was two weeks overdue. How could she have forgotten? Because she'd been so over the moon and in love? But how could it have happened?

She cast her mind back and it nearly broke her heart to recall the one time she'd had unprotected sex with Reith—a joyful coming together that had taken them both by surprise and then, she'd reassured herself, it wasn't the right time of the month for her to fall pregnant. So much for that theory, she thought. This was the reality and the shock of it was huge.

So that was why she'd been so uneven lately, so up, so down over nothing sometimes. Starving sometimes—she'd eaten two slices of Mary's carrot cake that morning—then unable to face food.

She sank into an armchair, mentally reeling from the impact of two huge revelations, then sat up precipitously. Was that why he didn't want any more children?

Did he view their marriage more as an affair, outside of which he could pursue another life?

Was it because of wretched Chilli George that he didn't want her, Kim, to have children? She covered her face with her hands and thought, distraught, that any woman other than Chilli George would not be quite so bad, but knew immediately she was kidding herself.

'Oh, Reith,' she whispered aloud, 'how could you do this to me? But don't think I'm going to take it lying down!' And she crossed to the phone.

'Ma'am, there's the red-eye flight,' the reservation clerk on the other end of the line told Kim. 'It leaves at midnight and gets into Brisbane at six thirty-five a.m. their time. You should be able to make it if you get to the airport shortly. We need a few extra minutes to process your dog.'

'I'll take it,' Kim responded.

The next day she sat on a veranda deck in Queensland, with an arm over Sunny Bob.

She was on the other side of the continent from Saldanha and Balthazar, from her parents, from Damien and, most especially, from Reith.

Most especially Reith because that hurt the most.

She'd hired a car and hunted around for accommodation that took pets, not that easy to find, so she'd kept driving. And, on a whim, she'd taken the car ferry across Moreton Bay, off Brisbane, to Russell Island, where, by chance, she'd found a house for rent where

Sunny Bob was welcome. It was also fully furnished and well-supplied with linen and everything she could need.

She'd paid the bond and a week's rent in advance and been invited to move right in with no further questions asked.

'You'll love it,' she'd been assured. 'Just watch out for the sandflies.'

Bearing that warning in mind, she'd stopped at the supermarket for some insect repellent as well as some essential supplies.

She'd been almost dead with tiredness by the time she'd let herself into the house and she hadn't taken much notice of it or the surroundings. She'd put the cold stuff in the fridge and collapsed on a sofa in the lounge.

She'd slept for hours.

Two days later, she was not only more alert, but she knew a bit more about her surroundings.

Her house was perched on a cliffside. The cliff ran down to what looked like a river but was called the Canaipa Passage and was the body of water that ran between Russell Island and North Stradbroke Island.

North Stradbroke rose across the water, uninhabited, opposite her house, and the birdlife was amazing. There were Brahminy kites with their deep bronze backs and wings, their snowy heads and their high free calls. There was a pair of White-breasted Sea Eagles that lived in the dark green jumble of foliage on a huge tree across the Canaipa. There were cormorants and shags, pelicans that paddled past, egrets and herons and black and white oyster catchers with their red beaks and legs. Thanks to a coffee-table book about Moreton Bay and a pair of binoculars, she was able to identify most of them. She could also see fish jumping in the water and wallabies foraging on the opposite shore.

She could identify the mangrove trees that lined the shores on both sides of the passage. And, despite her precautions, she'd received a couple of sandfly bites and found them almost intolerably itchy.

Life on Russell Island was easy-going and laid-back. A lot of the locals had boats and were keen fishermen. And she'd walked as she tried to come to terms with what she'd done. What she'd lost.

She'd sent a couple of text messages, one for her parents assuring them she was fine, one for Mary Hiddens saying the same. Then her phone had died and she realized she didn't have the charger with her.

On the night of her second day, a full moon rose over North Stradbroke Island and the colours of its great blood-orange orb and then, as it got higher, the pearl-pale radiance of the light it shed had been little short of miraculous.

All the same, Kim had found herself sobbing suddenly because it was all so beautiful and she was so alone and so devastated.

Sunny Bob put an anxious paw on her lap and she wrapped her arms around his neck and wept into his fur.

'The thing is,' she told him as she sat up and fished in her pocket for a tissue, 'I don't know if I did the right thing. I came away because I just couldn't bear to go back to the old hostilities that existed between me and Reith. But is that cowardly? Am I hoping in my heart of hearts that, despite all the precautions I took—and the fact that this is probably the last place he'd come looking for me—he will look?'

But why was he a womanizer anyway?

Her tearful thoughts slipped back to the night of Pippa Longreach's barbecue, the night she and Reith had first made love, but, before that, he'd told her why he was the way he was, then he'd demonstrated how implacable he could be.

How his mother's defection and his father's own brand of implacability and cynicism had shaped him. And through that confession she'd come to understand a little better the complex person who was Reith Richardson. It had to explain why it was hard for him to let anyone get too close. He'd even acknowledged that his first marriage had suffered from the exclusion zone without altogether acknowledging it.

Was this his way of maintaining that zone? By letting no one woman get too close to him?

She sat back and Sunny Bob settled at her feet.

'Anyway, lovely as it is, I can't sit around on Russell Island twiddling my thumbs for ever. What was I thinking?'

She answered her own question after a while. 'Not straight, just not able to face Reith.'

As for rushing into hasty decisions—was that what pregnancy did to you?

She got up and wandered out onto the deck.

Sunny Bob heaved a sigh but got up and followed her.

Not as cool as it was at home, nevertheless winter in Southern Queensland was chilly overnight and she drew her jumper more closely around her and folded her arms protectively over her belly at the same time as she thought—this should be such a joyous moment. I would love to have Reith's baby. Would he love to have our baby, though? And what about the 'other woman'?

'All the same, I think I'll have to go back.'

Her words seemed to echo as she stared out into the darkness.

There were ragged windy clouds partly obscuring the moon now and a south-easterly blowing up the passage. Twenty-five to thirty knots predicted for tomorrow, she recalled from watching the weather forecast on the TV news.

She shook her head, as if to say to herself, *concentrate!* and she repeated, 'I think we'll have to go back. I can't stay here for ever anyway and I need to sort things out, I need to make plans, I need to come back to earth…'

CHAPTER TEN

HER car was still parked in the long-term parking area at Perth Airport and not long after she'd landed she was driving down the Kwinana Freeway towards home, conducting a conversation with Sunny Bob.

'I've gone to a lot of trouble on your behalf,' she told him. 'It's not that easy to fly dogs around the country—actually it's easier to fly them than it is to do much else with them.'

Sunny Bob, curled up in the passenger seat, glanced at her reproachfully.

'Not that I'm holding anything against you,' she hastened to assure him. 'I don't know what I would have done without you. You've been a super friend.'

She patted him and grimaced because her nerves were jangling again. And concentrated on what she was going to say to Reith when she arrived at Saldanha.

Take hold, she advised herself. Don't, for heaven's sake, scream and shout at him. Don't get all emotional. Just tell him the truth. Tell him about the baby? Maybe. Maybe not yet…

But Reith wasn't there when she arrived home. Mary

was there and she gasped and burst into tears when she saw Kim.

'Oh, you shouldn't have, Kim,' she kept saying. 'We were so worried. Your parents…'

Kim comforted her as best she could and then asked the question that was burning on her brain. 'Where's Reith? Is he home? I believe he—'

'Reith,' Mary said with unmistakable venom. 'He's moved out and good riddance.'

Kim's mouth fell open at this absolutely uncharacteristic malice on the part of Mary.

'Where to?' she asked tonelessly.

'I don't know and I don't care,' Mary said militantly. 'Clover Hill, I believe. Oh, Kim…'

Kim hugged her again. 'Is he there now?'

'That I truly don't know. He could be but there've been all sorts of comings and goings. I believe he's here, there and everywhere.'

Kim went upstairs, where she showered and changed.

It was close to dusk and she put on a navy tracksuit and flat shoes. She left her hair loose with two wings pinned at the back. She put on no make-up other than lipgloss, but she sprayed a little perfume on. She noticed that her hands were shaking.

But, ready as she was, she still couldn't bring herself to go to Clover Hill. And she found herself wandering around the house, touching this and that, the old, old South African pieces, the silver- and copper-ware Mary kept so shiny. The lovely porcelain her grandmother had collected.

And she smiled at her renovations and how well she'd blended the new with the old. But the smile faded and a curious frown took its place. The old satisfaction she'd got from Saldanha and all its elegance, all its history seemed to have faded. In fact it seemed to have given way to a…what?

She looked around the lounge and realized what it was. A shivery little feeling woven in with the pleasure that told her the memories were mixed now; some were even memories she'd rather forget. It wasn't an entirely peaceful aura to Saldanha now.

She shook her head and wondered if she was being fanciful—and knew she could delay no longer.

Her car was in the garage but for once Sunny Bob looked less than enthusiastic about accompanying her.

She laughed. 'Have I taken all the wanderlust out of you, Sunny? OK, you can stay at home. I might be back soon myself, anyway.'

There were some lights on at Clover Hill but no one came to greet her when she parked opposite the front door.

There was a familiar gun-metal four-wheel drive parked on the gravel, though, and her nerves tightened.

But she forced herself to walk up to the front door and knock. There was no response, however.

Kim fought an almost overwhelming urge to run back to her car and drive away.

She tried the front door and it opened soundlessly under her hand. She took a very deep breath and walked in. There were lamps on in the lounge and one of the

French windows was open to the veranda. There was an untasted, by the look of it, glass of brandy on a side table.

'Anyone home?' she called softly.

There was no reply and something drew her to the open door to the terrace.

She stepped out into the darkness, made fragrant by the rose garden, and stopped dead as a tall figure loomed out of the twilight—Reith.

He stopped too and they simply stared at each other for an age. He wore jeans and a navy sweater. His hair was ruffled and his jaw was dark as if he hadn't shaved.

Then Kim made herself breathe normally and swallowed a couple of times. 'Reith,' she said huskily, 'I saw you with Chilli George in Perth a few nights ago. That's why I ran away. What was I doing in Perth? Not spying on you. I went up to see Damien, but that's another story.' She stopped abruptly as it struck her she'd forgotten about her brother in all the rest of it.

'I…' She put a hand up to her brow as she realized she felt a bit peculiar and wondered if her aversion to food was catching up with her. 'I…I mean you…well…' But she stopped again and this time her knees buckled and she would have fallen if he hadn't lunged forward and caught her.

The next few minutes were confused.

He picked her up in his arms and took her inside to lay her gently down on a settee. 'Stay there,' he warned.

She closed her eyes but it seemed like only moments later that he was back with a glass of brandy that he held to her lips.

She took a sip then pushed the glass away vehemently and sat up. 'No—'

'Kim,' he said quietly, 'it will help. Just—'

'No! No,' she said, 'you don't understand! I can't drink alcohol!'

'Why not?' He frowned.

'Because I'm…I'm…' She couldn't go on.

She saw the understanding that came to his eyes. 'Pregnant?'

'Yes.' Sudden tears streamed down her face. 'And on top of seeing you with another woman, a woman I *hate*, incidentally, I have no idea whether you want us to have children or if Darcy is the only family you want or if it's because of her you don't want more children—or what!' She couldn't go on as her throat started to hurt unbearably and she put her hand up to it.

He pulled up a chair and sat down facing her. 'Where were you?'

Her eyes widened. 'I… Queensland. A place called Russell Island.'

'Never heard of it.'

'Neither had I. It was…interesting and very peaceful. Reith,' she breathed, 'I—'

'I met Chilli,' he broke in and ran his hand gently over her hair, 'in the hotel lobby that evening. We bumped into each other, had a brief conversation—she asked after you, as a matter of fact. Then she said she had a taxi waiting for her and she invited me to have dinner with her. I declined and walked her out to the car. That's where she did something I was not expecting, an intimate gesture, I guess you could call it.' He shrugged.

'Very intimate,' Kim said dryly.

'Very Chilli,' Reith responded, equally dryly. Then he added levelly, 'But not me, Kim. Not me.'

She stared at him.

'I swear to you that's all there was to it.'

'You seemed…to be much struck,' she said raggedly.

A grim little smile twisted his lips. 'You could say I got the surprise of my life. She's probably one of the most predatory women I've ever met. She's certainly not my type.'

Kim pushed herself upright. 'But, Reith, you don't want more children, do you? You… I could tell in the helicopter when I asked you, that you weren't keen and it wasn't just a matter of taking our time.'

'Kim…' He picked up her hand and seemed to battle for words for a moment. Then he said simply, 'It scares me.'

Kim blinked several times. 'Come again?'

'I've never quite forgiven myself for Sylvie's death. I couldn't bear it if the same thing happened to you. But tell me something, do *you* want this baby?'

There was a long pause as she searched his face, then she said steadily, 'Reith, more than anything in the world do I want your baby but—' she stopped and gestured helplessly '—I sometimes feel as if we're having an affair rather than being married.'

'That could be because—' He paused, then went on, 'Because I can't help wondering whether you're going to wake up one day and decide I'm not good enough for you.'

Her lips parted and her eyes were stunned. 'You… I don't believe it! Not you…' But, as she trailed off, thoughts of her brother Damien and his insecurities flashed across her mind.

'Really?' she said to Reith. 'Really, really?'

He took her hands in his. 'Really. In fact I thought that's what must have happened, that's why you'd run away.'

'No. Oh—' she grimaced '—I have to tell you, being pregnant does mysterious things to you. I've never made so many impetuous decisions in my entire life.'

He smiled but it faded and he rubbed the blue shadows on his jaw. 'I also wondered if you'd found out that I'd sold.'

'Sold?' she echoed.

He nodded.

'Sold what?'

He took a deep breath and his eyes never left her face. 'Saldanha and Balthazar.'

She gasped. 'What?' she whispered.

He nodded and saw the shock in her eyes. 'Kim,' he said intensely, 'there was never going to be any hope for us with those two thorny issues for ever between us. You were always going to be torn between me and your family.'

'I…I…' But she couldn't go on.

'If it's any consolation, they've gone to a South African consortium expanding their operations into

Western Australia. And they're happy to have your father on their board in an advisory capacity.'

Kim licked her lips. 'When did you do this?'

'It's been in the pipeline for a couple of months.'

'So you were thinking back then—even back then about me being torn?' she queried, her eyes huge with surprise.

'Yep.' He looked wry. 'You would have thought that might have alerted me to the way things stood for me regarding you.'

Kim stared at him. 'Mary,' she said agitatedly then. 'She's cross—she's *more* than cross with you! I don't understand. Why should she…?' She stopped.

He sighed. 'That's all my fault. When she told me you'd left with a bag and Sunny Bob but no hint of where you were going other than Perth, I told her, not pleasantly, that she should have stopped you. She then told *me* some home truths and—' he gestured '—we haven't got around to forgiving each other yet.'

Kim frowned. 'What home truths?'

'Along the lines of how I wasn't fit to kiss your feet, how she'd often wanted to strangle me because I was making you miserable.' He shrugged. 'That kind of thing.'

Kim put her glass down and the faintest shadow of a smile touched her mouth.

'You have no idea,' he continued gravely, but there was a little glint in his dark eyes that made her heart beat faster, 'the obstacles I've had to conquer for your fair hand, Kim Richardson.'

'Perhaps I can guess,' she said barely audibly. 'My

dog, my family and even my housekeeper. Oh, I forgot about causing you nearly to collide with a tree.'

'Kim.' His voice was unsteady and he stood up and this time there was a question in his eyes as he looked down at her.

Kim stood up slowly—and she flew into his arms. 'Oh, Reith, I love you! I've been so miserable, so…'

But he stopped her with his mouth on hers and he held her as if he'd never let her go.

'About Saldanha,' Reith said quite a bit later.

He'd lit a fire in the grate and closed the doors on the chill of the evening. He was sitting on the couch with her on his lap and he was slowly running his fingers through her hair.

'Mmm?' She looked up at him.

'Do you mind very much?'

Kim considered. 'No,' she said at last. 'I probably would have liked to think of a Theron always associated with Balthazar but you can't have everything.' She paused. 'Saldanha, though—I don't know how to describe it—but it doesn't seem to offer me peace any more, whereas this place does.' She looked around a little wonderingly.

'That's how I feel. As if we can leave all the trauma behind us and start afresh here.'

Hours later, she stirred in his arms.

The main bedroom had been furnished since she'd last seen it. It had a fireplace and there were glowing coals in the grate making flickering shadows on the walls. They lay beneath a light-as-air, warm-as-toast quilt.

'This Russell Island place,' he said, spanning her waist with his hands, 'must be well off the beaten track.'

'It is a bit.' She described it then said, 'Why?'

'It explains why I hadn't, to date, found you.'

'You looked?'

'Uh-huh.'

'Well, I ended up there mostly due to Sunny Bob—' She broke off and sat up. 'I told him I'd be back soon. Probably.'

The quilt slipped off her shoulders, revealing her to be naked to the waist. He removed his hands from her waist and cupped her breasts.

'He and Mary can console each other.'

Kim put a hand to her mouth. 'Her too! She'll be wondering.'

He plucked her nipples gently. 'Kim, they'll be fine.'

She took an unexpected breath. 'That's…not fair,' she breathed as she looked down at his strong hands on her breasts. She lay back and tremors of rapture and desire flowed down her body.

'I don't see what's unfair about it,' he replied.

'Well, we've already done this once tonight,' she reasoned.

'Who's counting?' he drawled and removed his hand from her breasts, only to start kissing them.

'Now that—' she had to take a very deep breath '—is very unfair. However, there's an old saying—what's sauce for the gander is sauce for the goose.'

He lifted his head and laughed down at her. 'It's the other way around.'

'Believe me, it can work both ways,' she advised as she trailed her fingertips down the hard wall of his chest, and lower.

It was his turn to suck in an unexpected breath and he swept her into his arms as they laughed together. Then he released her, but only to stare down at the sapphire-blue of her eyes, her red-gold hair, her lovely skin gilded in the firelight.

'Don't leave me again,' he growled.

'I won't,' she promised, and they made love for the second time.

CHAPTER ELEVEN

NEARLY eight months later, Darcy said, 'Wow, Kim, she's really, *really* tiny!' as he gingerly held a baby wrapped in a pink shawl.

'They usually are,' Reith murmured.

'Well, I knew that but—oh, she's going to cry. Here.' Darcy handed the little bundle hastily back to Kim, who was sitting propped up in bed in the same hospital where her friend Penny had had her baby—a baby that had, in a sense, thrown Kim Theron and Reith Richardson together.

Kim laughed as she took her newborn daughter back. 'No, she's not, she's just pulling a face. OK, guys! What are we going to call her?'

Reith looked down at her with his lips twitching. 'If I'm any judge, you've decided that yourself.'

Kim grimaced. 'I do have some ideas but I'm open to suggestions.'

Darcy looked at his father. Reith looked at his son.

Darcy said, 'We might as well let her decide. Saves time.'

'Yep,' Reith concurred.

Kim sat up, looking indignant. 'If you're suggesting that I always like to get my own way—'

'Always,' her husband and stepson broke in to agree.

Her expression defied description for a moment but the baby made a soft little gurgle and Kim looked down at her with a different expression entirely, one of such warmth and radiance that it nearly took Reith's breath away.

'Well,' she said, 'I suspect you'll attract a lot of names, sweetheart, *like* sweetheart, sweet pea, honey bunny, sugar bush, gorgeous—but to me you look like a Martha.'

Later, when they were alone, Kim said softly, 'You can relax now. There are no problems, no unforeseen complications.' But at the same time she blinked away some tears.

Reith looked a question at her.

'I was thinking of her.'

He sat on the bed and put his arms around her and they were quiet together in silent tribute to Darcy's mother.

Three months later, Martha Richardson was fast asleep, just, in her cot under the watchful eye of Mary Poppins, when her mother, dressed in a strapless sapphire gown that matched her eyes, descended the staircase at Clover Hill.

There was a spontaneous round of applause from the people grouped in the lounge. It was her birthday and her parents were there, Fiona in poppy-pink and looking young and almost as elegant as her daughter; Frank Theron looking distinguished in a dinner suit.

Damien was there with the same blonde, Lavinia, Kim had seen him with at the races. They'd recently married and Lavinia wore the most amazing silver dress that moulded, and hid very little of, her figure. Her hair was dyed platinum, her nails and lips were painted black and she wore a quantity of rhinestones in flamboyant jewellery. In spite of all this, she and Kim had made friends and Kim had decided that she was a shrewd, practical person and she certainly seemed to have turned Damien round.

Reith and Damien could not be described as mates, as Reith had predicted, but at least they mixed with an apparent lack of hostility nowadays, and it was the same with her father and Reith. Her mother, who'd always had plenty of respect for Reith, was now completely won over.

Pippa Longreach was there, in all shades of peacock-blue. She'd ditched Lachlan and gone to the other extreme, a man thirty years older but with a lot—make that a *lot*, she'd assured Kim—of money.

Bill and Molly Lawson were there.

Darcy was there, combed and ferociously clean.

And there was Reith, looking impossibly, darkly attractive in his dinner suit and snowy shirt, watching her come down in a way that made her stumble slightly.

How does he do it? she wondered. How does he still manage to make me feel sexy just by looking at me?

'Sorry,' she said lightly, 'I didn't mean to keep you waiting but Miss Martha has only just decided to go to sleep. Hello, Mum.' She walked up to her mother and hugged her. 'You look wonderful.'

'So do you, sweetheart, happy birthday!'

It was a happy dinner.

Mary Hiddens had forgiven Reith and moved over to Clover Hill, and she excelled herself on Kim's birthday dinner.

Then, just after the dessert had been cleared, Martha woke up, but not because she was cold, wet or hungry. So Kim brought her downstairs, where she put on, for a three-month-old, a bravura performance, smiling, gurgling and absolutely captivating all the guests.

'I'm not sure that this is such a good idea,' Kim said rather ruefully to Reith.

He looked down at her, 'Well, I've got the feeling she's going to be as much of a show-stopper as her mother.'

'I am not,' Kim denied.

'You are and I adore you for it,' he said quite casually, as if he was talking about the price of eggs. 'For example, if you hadn't danced into the middle of the road exposing your legs, I might never have met you.'

'You're never going to let me forget that, are you?'

He shrugged. 'Possibly not. Look at that,' he added with a smile in his voice as he gestured.

Kim looked in the direction he'd indicated and her eyes fell on Darcy, now holding his half-sister with a lot more confidence. If there was one person Martha loved above all, it was Darcy.

Kim felt a wonderful, warm glow flow through her

as she watched the baby and the boy. Now that's an achievement, she thought.

'What's this?' she said to Reith when all the guests had gone home, when Darcy was asleep and Martha was too, and Mary had closed herself into her own quarters.

'You may not have noticed but I didn't give you a birthday present,' he replied.

They were sitting on the veranda in the moonlight with the heady scent of the roses around them, having an Irish coffee. They had a candle in a glass on the table beside them.

'You've given me so much, Reith! I don't need a birthday present.'

'Yes, you do,' he contradicted. 'You need this, anyway.' And he put a velvet box tied with silver ribbon down on the table beside her.

Kim drew a careful breath, untied the ribbon and flicked open the box.

It was a ring, an exquisite square sapphire surrounded by diamonds on a gold band.

Reith got up and took the ring out of the box. Then he lifted her left hand and slipped it onto her ring finger on top of her wedding band.

She stared down at it, then looked up at him, and she didn't resist when he pulled her to her feet.

'Thank you,' she said huskily. 'It's beautiful.'

He drew her into his arms and said against her hair, 'I wish I could tell you how much I love you.'

'You have. You do.'

'So that you believe me, I mean. So that you never feel you have to run away because I don't love you.'

'Reith, I believe you,' she said, then smiled up at him. 'I really, *really* believe you.'

* * * * *

Save over £40

Join the Mills & Boon Book Club

Subscribe to **Modern™** today for 3, 6 or 12 months and you could **save over £40!**

'e'll also treat you to these fabulous extras:

- **FREE L'Occitane gift set worth £10**
- **FREE home delivery**
- **Books up to 2 months ahead of the shops**
- **Bonus books, exclusive offers... and much more!**

Subscribe now at

vww.millsandboon.co.uk/subscribeme

'sit us
'nline

Save over £40 – find out more at
www.millsandboon.co.uk/subscribeme

SUBS/OFFER/P

Have Your Say

You've just finished your book. So what did you think?

We'd love to hear your thoughts on our 'Have your say' online panel
www.millsandboon.co.uk/haveyoursa

- Easy to use
- Short questionnaire
- Chance to win Mills & Boon® goodies

Tell us what you thought of this book now at
www.millsandboon.co.uk/haveyoursay